·SIEGMUND·THE·
·WÖLSUNG·

The Valkyries

*The flight of
the Valkyries.*

The Valkyries

BY

E. F. BENSON

Author of
"Limitations," "Dodo," etc.

E. F. BENSON

Edward Frederic Benson was born at Wellington College (where his father was headmaster) in Berkshire, England in 1867. He was educated at Marlborough College, where he proved himself as an excellent athlete, representing England at figure skating, and published his first novel, *Dodo* (1893), when he was 26. The novel was quite popular, and Benson eventually expanded it into a trilogy (*Dodo the Second*, in 1914, and *Dodo Wonders*, in 1921). Nowadays, Benson is principally known for his 'Mapp and Lucia' series about Emmeline "Lucia" Lucas and Elizabeth Mapp. The series consists of six novels and two short stories, and remains popular to this day, being serialized for Radio 4 as recently as 2008. Benson was also a respected writer of ghost stories – indeed, H. P. Lovecraft spoke very highly of him, especially his story 'The Man Who Went Too Far'. Benson died of throat cancer in 1940, aged 72.

WALTRAVTE

CONTENTS

Contents

ILLUSTRATIONS

PREFACE

In the following pages an attempt has been made to render as closely as possible into English narrative prose the libretto of Wagner's *Valkyries*. The story is one little known to English readers, and even those who are familiar with the gigantic music may find in the story something which, even when rendered into homely prose, will reveal to them some new greatness of the master-mind of its author. It is in this hope that I have attempted this version.

Whether I have attempted a task either absolutely impossible, or impossible to my capacity, I cannot tell, for so huge is the

scale of the original, so big with passion,
so set in the riot of storm-clouds and
elemental forces, that perhaps it can only
be conveyed to the mind as Wagner
conveyed it, through such sonorous musical
interpretations as he alone was capable of
giving to it.   Yet even because the theme
is so great, rather than in spite of it, any
interpretation, even that of halting prose,
may be unable to miss certain of the force
of the original.

The drama itself comes second in the
tetralogy of the Ring, being preceded by
the Rheingold.   But this latter is more
properly to be considered as the overture
to a trilogy than as the first drama of a
tetralogy.   In it the stage is set, and
Heaven above, rainbow-girt Walhalla, and
the dark stir of the forces beneath the earth,
Alberich and the Niebelungs, enter the

arena waiting for the puny and momentous
sons of men to assert their rightful lordship
over the earth, at the arising of whom the
gods grow grey and the everlasting foundations of Walhalla crumble.   From the
strange loves of Siegmund and Sieglinde,
love not of mortal passion, but of primeval
and elemental need, the drama starts ; this
is the first casting of the shuttle across the
woof of destiny.   From that point, through
the present drama, through Siegfried,
through the dusk of the gods the eternal
grinding of the mills continues.   Once set
going the gods themselves are powerless
to stop them, for the stream that turns
them is stronger than the thunderings of
Wotan, for the stream is "That which
shall be."

   In storm the drama begins, in storm of
thunder and all the range of passion and

B

of death it works its inevitable way, till for a moment there is calm, when on the mountain-top Brunnhilde sleeps, waiting for the coming of him whose she is, for the awakening to the joy of human life. And there till Siegfried leaps the barrier of flame we leave her.

E. F. BENSON.

THE VALKYRIES

CHAPTER I

INTRODUCTION

THE HOUSE OF HUNDING

NEVER before in the memory of man had spring been so late in coming, and into mid-May had lasted the hurricanes and tempests of winter. Not even yet was the armoury of its storms and squalls wholly spent, and men, as they huddled by the fire and heard night by night, and day by day the bugling of the wind, and the hiss of rain and the patter of the hailstones, wondered what this subversion and stay of the wholesome seasons should portend.

For now for many years had strange
omens and forebodings shadowed and
oppressed the earth. Some said that the
earth itself and Erda the spirit of earth
were growing old ; some even had seen the
great mother, not as of old she had appeared from time to time, vigorous and
young, clad in the fresh green of growing
things, but old and heavy-eyed, and her
mantle was frosted over with rime, for the
chill of the unremitting years had fallen
on her. Others again said that in
Walhalla, which Wotan the father of gods
and men had builded by the might of
giants, all was not well ; that shadows
crowded in places where no shadows
should be, and that their companies grew
ever greater, and that dim voices of wailing
and of warning sounded in the ears and
in the high places of the gods. Others

said that the gods themselves were growing old ; that Wotan feared the spirits of
the earth, and of the places beneath the
earth, for he was no longer certain of his
strength, and that age and the grey shadow
of death itself looked over his shoulder
when he sat alone, and when he slept with
Fricka his wife visions of ill portent would
trouble his dreams so that often he rose at
dead of night from his couch, and would
look from the walls of Walhalla over the
still sleeping earth, wondering from which
quarter danger would come, and from
where he would first see the red light of
war. Night by night he would commune
with himself, wondering how it was that
the strength and the merriment of old days
had departed, wondering, yet in himself
knowing. For he knew the Book of Fate
and of that which should be, as a man still

dreaming knows that he is in bed, and the
night-hag rides him, and yet is powerless
either to fully sleep or fully wake.   Certain
also it was that day by day he sent his
daughters, whom he begat by Erda the
spirit of the earth, to slay and bring into
Walhalla heroes of the sons of men, into
whom he breathed the spirit of eternal life
so that for ever they should guard those
walls that once he thought impregnable ;
and day by day did the eight Valkyries,
led by Brunnhilde, the fairest and the
strongest of them all, go on their quests.
She it was in whom above all Wotan delighted, for so at one with him was the
swift strength and fearless will of the maid ;
it was to her he told all his intentions and
his purposes, and not to Fricka his wife,
so that often when he talked with Brunnhilde he scarcely knew whether he spoke to

her or whether his own soul but communed
with itself. Yet though he thus guarded
Walhalla, thinking to make it safe, he knew
that there was one thing in the world which
was stronger than he, and that was Fate.
What Should Be, would be, and What
Should Be recked of Wotan as lightly as it
recked of the falling of a sparrow, or the
passing of a spring shower.

Now these omens of gloom and fate
which lay heavy on Walhalla, troubled also
the minds of men. If death came to the
gods, should not death come also to the
earth and the children of the earth? When
the Master fell should not the servant fall
also? Yet because the race of men were
yet but young on the earth, and vigorous,
flourishing in stony places like a creeping
plant that shall soon cover the desert
with its stems, there were men, and those

wise ones, who held that after the fall of
the gods the kingdoms of the world and all
the sovereignty of the earth should soon be
given to the sons of men.   And they looked
for the coming of one who should challenge
the gods themselves, before whom the
everlasting foundations of Walhalla should
crumble.   He it was, they said, whom
Wotan feared, he who was free and owed
nothing to the lords of Walhalla, for Wotan
knew that before him his own god-like
strength would crumble as a dead leaf, and
as a dead leaf be borne away on the winds.
And in this long continuance of winter,
when already spring should have awakened
the earth with its glad shout, they saw in
figure the winter of the gods; and when
winter should cease and spring come, even
so would come in the fulness of time now
nigh the upspringing of men, in which

should be forgotten the winter of the gods. For the finger of fate pointed to the new time, when Walhalla should be shaken and fall, and men should be slaves no longer to the early outworn gods, but possess the earth in peace and plenty.

Yet still in mid-May the storms of winter were not spent; still the sap of growing things stayed and stirred not in the barren branches of the forest trees. And winter still froze and hardened in the heart of Sieglinde the wife of Hunding. Though she had been long his wife, yet she was still young, and her woman's heart hungered for love, and starved for a man she could love, but froze again ever into ice at the sight of her lord. Unwittingly and by compulsion of her kindred and his she had married him; hate blossomed in her heart where the flower of love should have made fragrance, and in all but deed she was unfaithful to him. Day by day she did the work of a wife ; she made his food for him before he went out to the hunt, whether it was the deer he hunted to make venison, or man that he hunted for vengeance, for he was of the tribe of the Niedings, who wooed by sword and violence, and from the slaughter of her kindred had often borne away a maid to her wedding feast. Then after she had given him his food, she would give him his spear and sword and shield, a service which but earned her a curse or a blow, and watch him stride off into the forest, with bitter loathing in her heart. And truly if hate could kill, Hunding would have died by his wife's hand a hundred deaths a day.

But the hours when he was out were more tolerable, for after she had cleaned the house, and made all ready for his return, she would be free of the man she so hated till night came. Then, maybe, if suns were fair, she would sit outside the house, listening to the sounds of the forest at noonday, little knowing how in the years that were coming, one, her first-born and only son, of a stranger union than ever gods or men had dreamed of, would listen in like manner to the murmurs of the forest, till the song of the bird spoke to him not with unintelligible twitterings, but with a voice as clear as the tones of a friend. Or she would let down her mane of golden hair, loving it because it was beautiful, and hating it because it was Hunding's, his to twine passionate hands in, his to cut off and throw on to the hearth if so he wished. Thus she both hated and loved her own beauty ; loved it because she longed to give it to a man she loved, hated it because it belonged to a man she hated.

At other times she would walk down through the pine-trees to where the mountain brook fell into the black lake, that lay deeper, it was said, than line could plumb. Often she had sat there, wondering how it was that she of the Wolsung breed, daughter of the god Wotan, when in form of a man he wooed and won the forest maid who was her mother, yet lacked the courage to plunge in and be done with Hunding and her woe for ever. Yet had she known it, it was courage not cowardice that held her back from the leap, courage and that firm and strong belief that burned like a little flame, so clear, and yet so tiny within her, that there was something more written for her in the Book of Fate, to which even

*Often had sh.
sat there.*

Wotan bowed, than that she should end
all in one moment of unwomanly despair.
Then, maybe, she would creep to the edge
of the water, where the lake lay still and
windless, and behold in that mirror the
wonder and glory of her face, warm and
red with the flow of her strong blood, with
the great grey eyes all wildness and all
fierce passion for the man she had never
seen, whose coming her heart welcomed.

"Surely I bring him a gift which not
many would despise," she would say to
herself; "and O, when he comes, the
love which is in my heart will make me
more beautiful than ever!" Then, maybe,
if the spring stirred in her blood, she
would lie there imagining him. Dark men
she hated, because Hunding was dark.
Dark was he and swarthy, of great stature,
but so broad of build that he seemed not

tall.   Dark eyes looked from out of the
eaves of his overhanging brows, a cavern
fringed with long growth of eyebrows, and
dark and mirthless and cruel was his heart.
Not so should her lover be ; he, the man
for whom fate had predestined her, for
whose sake fate held her back from the
lake that was as black as Hunding.   No,
he should be tall, but slight, strong with
the strength of speed and lightness, not
strong with the knotted strength of the oak-
tree.   Hunding was black, so he should
be fair, his hair of the colour of honey
when it is drained fresh from the nest of
the wild bee, and the sun strikes it.

"Yes, yes," she would say, "the colour,
the colour ;" and then a braid of her own
hair would stray over her shoulder ; "yes,
that colour," she would say ; and indeed it
was beyond compare, for fresh honey was

lustreless beside it. Grey should his eyes be, for Hunding was dark, grey with a reflected blueness lying deep therein, even as her own eyes were grey like thin skeins of cloud suffused with the inimitable blue of the heaven behind them. Then she would picture him, and lo! when the picture was complete, the man whom she desired, for whom her heart waited, was of the same glorious mould as herself, such a man as Wotan might have begotten by the forest maiden who bore Sieglinde herself.

Then when evening approached and the shadows of the pines began to lengthen across the lake, and the twittering of birds began to be hushed in the bushes, she would turn homewards again, and get ready the supper for her lord, and wait his return. Sometimes even when she gazed into the lake, his image would cross her mind, and

c

at that the reflection of her face froze and
sickened.   And every evening when she
heard his step it froze and sickened, and
her heart sickened also, and Sieglinde was
Sieglinde no longer, but his wife, faithless
in all but deed.   Sometimes if the day and
work had not gone well, he would speak no
word to her, and again a curse or a blow
might be her only traffic with him till next
day he went forth again into the forest.
But if the day had prospered with him, if he
had slain much game, be it man or beast,
he would be well pleased with her, and
laugh to see her hatred of him, for that but
seemed to kindle his love for her beauty.
But Sieglinde was better pleased if he
cursed her, for since he was hateful to her,
his displeasure was almost sweet to her, but
his pleasure made her sometimes hot with
hatred against him, and she could have

killed him, sometimes cold with hatred, when she could have killed herself. Nevertheless, between her and death stood ever the image of one who should come with outpouring of love, at sight of whom her own love long frozen and pent within her, nor even yet come to birth, should also be outpoured as the sap in a tree is called forth by the spring and the sun, and must follow that sweet bidding. But as yet it was winter with her and the world, and for sun the chill rain hissed on the roof-tree, and among the trees of the forest the winter wind sighed in the bitter air.

The house of Hunding, Sieglinde's house of hate, stood high in the forest, and all round it grew great trees of stately growth, where in this May-time the birds should have been already mated, the male with throatfuls of song to while his mate's hour of patient brooding, she busy with the cares of motherhood. But so long had winter lingered, that the branches and boughs were still scarcely green with the buds that herald spring, and as yet their feathered citizens were silent. On the hill-side the pine forest came down to the borders of the stream which fed the lake into which Sieglinde used so often to look, and from year's end to year's end this was never wholly silent because of the breezes that even in the depth of summer made music in the pines, so high and open to the clear winds of heaven was the place set, and by night and day low moaning as of a distant sea sounded ever through the chambers of the house of Hunding. Four-square was the house; the door opened straight from the wood of beech and oak in which it stood, into the dwelling-place, and on one

side was the open hearth with seats right
and left of it.   When sitting there Sieglinde
could see through the smoke-hole the sky
outside, and on clear nights would notice
how the stars looked down through the
curling wood-smoke, even as that which
she knew would come to her shone steadfastly, though often obscured through the
troubled clouds of her life.   In front stood
the table at which Hunding ate, and at
which, when her lord had finished, she ate
also.   In the very centre of the hall grew
a great tree, in the branches of which
rested the beams of the roof.   This was
the work of Hunding, which he had pre-
pared before ever he went on his violent
wooing ; and cunningly was it contrived, so
that the strength and stability of the tree
passed into the house itself, and not all the
winds of heaven could move the house

unless the tree itself was uprooted.   Often
did Sieglinde gaze at the mighty trunk,
but not for pleasure at the workmanship of
the house, but because in her day-dreams
she ever saw her deliverance from the
hated yoke of Hunding bound up with the
tree.   For on the day of her abhorred
wedlock, when the kith and kin of Hunding made merry at his marriage feast,
while she, whom he had carried off, sat
apart with downcast eyes, and heart in
which hatred of her husband already had
flowered, there strode into the hall one
whom neither she nor Hunding, nor any
of those who sat at meat with him, knew.
But as he came into the hall, a hush fell
on the din of merry-making, and none
durst ask him who he was, or what his
business there might be.   First one and
then another started up to ask him what

he did there, for he came unbidden by any, but at the flash of his eye, each in turn fell back abashed, but Sieglinde met his gaze undismayed, and found there no tremor nor fear, but a sudden spring of hope. The stranger was clad in a long cloak of blue, and on his head was a hat of so wide a brim that one of his eyes only was seen. Yet that was enough to put fear into the hearts of all except Sieglinde, and she found there hope and the promise of delivery. Still in silence he drew the sword he wore, and with one movement buried it up to the hilt in the stem of the ash. Then said the stranger: "Whoso can pull out the sword, his shall it be," and without more words strode out as he had come. Then one after the other, beginning from Hunding, all tried to draw out the sword, yet none with his utmost

might could stir it an inch from the place
where the stranger had so lightly thrust it.
But ever, since the stranger's glance had
fallen on her, Sieglinde knew in her heart
that the man who would draw it out would
be her deliverer from the house of hate.
And thus she often cast her eyes to where
the hilt of the sword still gleamed against
the dark trunk of the ash, and waited for
one to come.

For the rest, curtains of woven wool,
the work of Sieglinde's years of loveless
marriage, hung on the walls, and on the
floor were strewn bear-skins, the spoils of
Hunding's hunting. Beside the hearth a
stairway of few steps led to the store-
house, and in the wall opposite was the
door that led to the bed-chamber. Little
recked Hunding when in the house of
aught but his food and his sleep; and the

table at which he ate, the stool on which
he sat, and the bed in which he slept were
furniture enough for him.   And since to
Sieglinde the house was a house of hate,
she cared not to make it fair as women do
whose heart is at home.   Clean was the
house and bare ; the roof kept out the
rain, and Hunding's hunting made a fat
table.

CHAPTER II

THE COMING OF THE STRANGER

On a certain day then in this May month, when winter still held sway, Hunding, as his custom was, had left the house armed with his spear and sword and shield, as soon as the eyelids of the wind-swept morning opened in the skies, and all day Sieglinde had been alone. All day too a riotous storm had beset the place, so that she had stirred not from the house, but when her work was done sat and listened to the bugling blasts, half in fear, half in hope that this tempest and hurly-burly of the skies might prove too strong for the cunning handiwork of

Hunding, and that the very house should fall upon her as she sat there, making an end of her hopes and her hate.   So strong was the tempest that she feared Hunding might return before the day was over, but the hours passed on, and still he came not ; and towards the sunset she went into the store-house, as her custom was, to make ready for his supper.

Shrill and loud blew the wind, so that the walls of the house trembled with its violence, and the sheets of rain were flung unceasingly against the building.   For all that, it seemed to her that by now some change had come over the day ; no longer were the blasts cold and piercing like those she had known now for months past, but there was something of warmth and softness in them.   And for all the rain was so heavy, yet to her mind it was more like to

the heavy and fruitful rain of spring than
the volleyings of winter tempests. All this
made within her a sort of eager restlessness ;
often during the day she had started on
some errand in her work, and had left it
with a sigh unfinished or had forgotten
what she had intended ; often too she had
looked at the sword-hilt gleaming against
the dark ash-stem, and thrills of unaccount-
able expectation had been hers suddenly
and unconjecturably sweet. But as the
day went on, the storm grew even
fiercer, though it seemed to her that a
warmth and languor was in the air, and
tardily enough and with limbs unstrung
she went about the time of sunset to the
store-house. The bread she had made
that morning was there, and the venison
which Hunding had killed two days
before. Then from the store she took

honey to make mead for his drink, when
suddenly she heard the house door bang,
and hate surged bitterly into her throat, for
she knew that it must be her husband
come home.   And whether it was the
coming of spring that troubled her blood
or not, she felt then for him such loathing
as had never before been hers, and her
hand so trembled that she stayed a little
within, till he should call to her, or until
she was more mistress of herself.   But no
sound came from the hall, and after a little
while, leaving the meat and the bread and
the honey there, she went to the door to
see whether it was indeed Hunding who
had returned, for she wondered that he had
not called to her.

It was now dark, and only the gleam
from the fire made a little brightness in
the hall, and for a moment she thought that

it must have been the wind only that had
moved the door, for she saw none there,
neither Hunding nor another, but only the
firelight crouching on the hearth and
leaping on the walls of the empty room,
and gleaming very brightly on the hilt of
the sword which the stranger had buried
in the ash-stem on the day of her marriage.
Then with a cry of surprise she saw that
a man was stretched out on the bear-skin
by the hearth, without movement, but
lying like one dead. His face she could
not see, for it was turned away from her
towards the fire, but he was tall in stature,
and his arm, bare to the shoulder, was
strong and sinewy. His clothes were
ragged and drenched with the rain, but
the firelight shone on the hair that fell
thickly to his shoulder, and it gleamed
yellow in the firelight like the honey she

had just now drawn for her husband's
mead. And when she saw that she felt
that for a moment a long-drawn breath
hung suspended in her bosom. Then, for
here was a man sick perhaps to death, and
in need of help, the thought that had not
yet been consciously hers died again, and
she went nearer to him. But still the man
did not move ; only she saw that his tunic
rose and fell with the rising and falling of
his breath, and she knew that whoever he
was he was not dead, but only fallen in
sore faintness of exhaustion, and that his
eyelids, which had fallen over his eyes, so
that the lashes swept his cheek, were not
closed in the sleep of death. And as she
thus looked at his face which was turned
towards the firelight, again a breath hung
suspended in her bosom, for he was fair,
not dark like Hunding, and the short

beard of early manhood which fringed his lip and covered his chin was yellow, even as the honey which she had drawn for her husband's mead.

Even as she looked, the man stirred, and though his eye did not open, his tongue moved in his mouth, and—

" Water, water ! " he whispered, and his voice was low and deep and soft.

At that Sieglinde stayed not in idle surmise, but pity for a man distressed woke in her heart, pity and the woman's need to help, and she took up Hunding's drinking-horn which she had laid on the table for his supper, and hurried out of the house to where the well of water sprang bubbling out of the mossy bed beneath the hawthorn trees. The storm had altogether ceased, and in the heaven washed clean by the rain the stars burned large. The chill of the long winter had gone, and the balmy warmth of spring filled the air, and, even as she bent to fill the horn at the runnel of water, close above her head a nightingale burst into bubbling song. And she wondered, yet paused not to wonder, but hurried back into the house with the horn brimful of the fresh spring water.

So with the horn in her hand she returned, and found the stranger still lying as she had left him, and into his nerveless hand she put the horn.

"Water," she said, "thou didst ask for water;" and he drank till the horn was empty, yet still raised not his eyes.

"Water, water," he said; "thou hast given me water, and I give thee thanks. Already——"

And he paused, and the bear-skin stood

D

away from the braced arm. " Already I am my own master again. That was all I needed."

Yet that was not all, for he sank back again to his elbow in the bear-skins, and he gazed at her.

" Lady, I thank thee," said he. " Thou hast wakened me, thou hast welcomed me. The sleep and darkness of my faintness stands away from me. So tell me : whom is it that I thank ? "

Just then the firelight died down, and from flame there was but a mere glow on the walls. Only in the darkness the glow lit on the hilt of the sword that a stranger on the day of her marriage feast had thrust in the ash-stem, and on the head of a stranger who lay at the hearth. Yet wondrously spring bubbled in her heart, though as yet she knew nought but that

" Lady, I thank thee."

T. Noyes
Lewis.

only a wayfarer had happened here, and that she had relieved his sore need.

" The house is Hunding's," said she. " She who gave thee drink is the wife of Hunding," and at that the hatred of her man rose bitter and deadly in her throat. " His guest—the guest of Hunding art thou. Abide then here, he will soon be home."

Thereat a sudden log caught fire in the hearth, and in the blaze she saw the colour fly to his face, and the light from the fire-light sparkle in his eyes. And they were grey, but blue was behind them, as if a summer cloud flecked the open heaven.

"There is no harm," said he, still weak from his adventure, and loth to meet her gaze ; " I am without weapon. He would not grudge a weaponless guest such harbourage, though his wife is alone with

him and tends to him.   Also I am
wounded."

"Wounded!" she cried; and again
there was nought but pity in a woman's
heart for a man in distress, pity and the
need to give help.   "Where art thou
wounded?   Let me see to thy hurt."

Again he raised his eyes to her, and at
the sight his blood beat quicker, and
resumed its more wonted way, and, refreshed of his faintness by the water she
had brought him, he shook the hair back
from his white forehead, and though not
yet enough himself to stand up, sat erect
on the bear-skin, rejoicing to feel the life
return in warmth and tingling to his limbs.
And he thought no more of his wounds,
for it was of the gracious woman who
faced him that he thought.

"Ah, they are nothing," he said.

"They are not worth the words we have already spent on them. See! my arms will serve me yet," and he thrust out first one and then the other with vigour, so that the muscles stood out on them like cords, and in turn he clenched his hands. "Would that my shield and spear had served me as well," said he; "then should I not have run from my foes, but my shield was shivered, and my sword broken. Yes, I am a man who ran from his foes. What else could I do? Often through the forest they were close behind me, and often the branches through which I plunged had not yet closed behind me, when one or another of my foes was lashed by the back-stroke of the twigs. But now, faster than my flight my faintness leaves me. Faster than the storm, which all day has buffeted me, riding on the wings of the wind, my strength returns; my fear and the night and darkness which closed over my senses roll away, and the sun comes out again."

Low burned the firelight on the hearth; and in the darkness she could scarce see the stranger's face, but the music of his voice beat on her ear, and within her, her heart beat in tune to it. And a sudden tumult shook her, and she sprang up, feeling the need to do something, not to watch only for the upspringing of the fire so that she should see him, nor to question him so that his voice should sound on her ear. So again she took the drinking-horn of Hunding, and fetched honey from the store-chamber, and made within it the yellow mead, and handed it him.

"Drink," she said. "The water has given thee life; take thy strength again also."

" Drink thou first," said he.

So Sieglinde took the horn and sipped it, and gave it back to the stranger. And he, putting his lips where hers had touched the horn, drank deeply of it, and bowing his head in thanks gave it back to her. As he did so, again the fire shot up and prospered on the hearth; each saw the other more clearly than before, and the woman was fair and the man also, and in each grey eyes were shot with blue, and the yellow hair of each was of the same brightness. Long they looked at each other undismayed, he, because he must soon depart, and this one long look could hurt neither, unless a little heart-ache were a hurt; she, because her dreams had become suddenly coloured with life, and because she hated Hunding.

But there comes an end to all moments

be they sweet or bitter, and soon he got up. Tall was he as Hunding, but his form was slight as of a youth but lately come to man's estate, but in the clean lines of arm and leg there was strength and swiftness.

" Thou hast refreshed my faintness," said he. " Thou hast given me life again. And for thanks what can I say ? This only : may sorrow ever be a stranger to thee. May happiness be ever about thy home. I am rested and refreshed ; I will go on my way."

Then her heart awoke, and told her that she could not let him go. Already the fire of love was beginning to burn within her, and her dreams every moment were flushed more deeply with life. And though her voice was half strangled in her throat, she answered him lightly : " Why such haste?" she said; "wait a little longer."

He paused on his foot and looked at her.

" That would be but poor thanks for thy kindness," said he; "for wherever I go I bring sorrow with me, sorrow and ill-luck. If thou wert my enemy I would stay; it is because thou hast been good to me and gracious that I go, taking my ill-luck with me, that it should not abide untowardly in thy house. So I delay not, but go," and he turned quickly and went to the door.

Then when his hand was on the latch, and in the next moment he would have gone forth into the night, and out of her sight for ever, her heart again would not suffer her to remain dumb. Little of sorrow or ill-luck could he bring to her while she abode still in the house of

Hunding, for all the sorrow in the world, or so it seemed to her, was hers already, nor was there any ill-luck which he could bring which should be comparable to that which was ever about her house and about her bed, and sat at meat with her.

" There is no sorrow thou couldest bring me," said she, "for it is mine already. Look on these walls; they are builded firm, and it is of hate they are builded. Sorrow and hate and ill-luck were the masons, and they have built well. Look! thou wilt find no cranny nor chink. O, I have a well-established house!" and she laughed with sudden bitterness. "So stay," she said, and her voice quivered like an aspen leaf.

By now the logs that Sieglinde had cast on the hearth against Hunding's return were fully caught, and loud laughed the

firelight on the walls.   In that brightness
they saw each other more clearly yet, and
the long look that had passed between
them was again renewed.   Other fires, too,
were burning, for each now felt much pity
for the other—Sieglinde for the stranger
in that he was lonely and the quarry of ill-
luck ; the stranger for her in that when
love should have been blossoming in her
home, the strong poisonous flowers of hate
were there instead.   But as she spoke, the
latch fell from his fingers, and he slowly
returned and sat down by the hearth.

"Yet I have warned thee," said he.
"Woe is my name, and if thou fearest not
Woe, thou fearest not me.   I will wait for
Hunding to thank him for the rest and
refreshment I have found in his house."

Then though Sieglinde's heart rejoiced
that she had stayed his going, yet she was

troubled.   For though nothing could have been more right than that he should wait for Hunding, her lawful lord, yet she knew why she had bade him stay, for the woman in her called for man.   And in silence she lit the lamp and placed it on the table; and in troubled silence she made all ready for Hunding's coming.   Not long did she wait, for in a short space she heard the stroke of his horse's hoofs on the stones without; she heard him lead the beast to the stable and shut the door; she heard his step again outside and the jar of the lifted latch.

Then she looked once more at the stranger and he at her, and with that the door opened, and Hunding, black as the night outside, stood there.   Then seeing a stranger by the hearth he paused, with the door still swung open, and looked with an unspoken question at his wife.   From without came in the warm breath of the spring night, and the dwelling-place was filled with it, as the vats are filled with the odours of the wine when the vintage time has come, and in the heart of Sieglinde the flowers of hate burst into passionate blossom, and with that growth was mingled another.

CHAPTER III

THE STORY OF THE STRANGER

FOR a moment there was silence. Then said Sieglinde : " I found him here by the hearth, Hunding ; he was faint, his foes pursued him."

Hunding looked darkly at her, and more darkly yet at the stranger. He on Hunding's entrance had turned himself, and risen from his seat, as if to greet his host ; but even as his greeting was on his lips he had paused, for there was something in that black look which made him feel some echo of Sieglinde's hate.

" It is ever well to help the helpless,"

said Hunding evilly. " Thou gavest him refreshment ? "

" Even so," said she. " He was my guest—your guest ; faint by the hearth I found him. He waited for your coming."

Not a smile of welcome did Hunding give, for it was not his way to smile ; and already in his black heart hatred blackened towards his guest, and suspicion, ere yet it came, cast its shadow. And as his host did not greet him, neither did the stranger greet his host. Yet he could not bear that the woman should be blamed for what he had done. His was the blame.

" I was shelterless," said he, looking at Hunding. " She sheltered me. I was faint : she revived me. Is there blame in that? "

" Blame ? Who talks of blame ? " said

E

Hunding more blackly yet. " My hearth is holy : not otherwise has any guest of mine found it, and guest of mine art thou. Inviolable are these laws."

And without more words he turned to Sieglinde, who, as her custom was, took his weapons of hunting and hung them up on the ash-tree beneath the gleaming sword-hilt. Hunding hated the sword-hilt, for he had not been able to move it, and he knew that in this world there was but one who could. On that day also he knew trouble would come to his house. But he told Sieglinde to bring supper for him and his guest, and as she moved about her work, he stood beneath the ash-stem and looked from her to the stranger and back again. Each was cast in noble mould, and they were strangely like the one to the other, for the head of each was

bright with sunny hair, and in the grey
eye of each was seated some secret sorrow.
Tall was his wife, and tall the stranger,
and the skin of each was fair as the skin of
a child, and as smooth. For himself he
felt like a base-born man in the presence
of the gently bred ; and as he looked he
hated each, and the shadow of his suspicion grew darker. Then he turned to
the stranger, and speaking like a man who
conceals nought—

"Thy way has been long," he said,
"and thou hast no horse. Where hast thou
come, and whither goest thou ? What
journey has thus travel-stained thee?"

Then said the stranger : "The storm
and the foe have driven me far, and by
what way I know not. And where I
have come I know not, for my way was
long, and the heavens and earth were

blinded with tempest. Tell me then where I have come."

And as Hunding looked on him again, the likeness of the stranger to his wife smote on him like a blow; and again he looked from one to the other, as Sieglinde brought in venison and the fresh-baked bread, and put them ready on the table. But he answered him with seeming frankness.

"It is to Hunding's house thou hast come," he said, "and under the roof of Hunding thou hast rested. Not here is the home of my kindred, but far away to northward; and they of my blood are mighty and many. Be seated then, guest of mine, and in return tell me thy name."

So the stranger seated himself, and when he was seated Hunding sat down also, and Sieglinde, who had finished the serving, sat by her husband opposite to their guest, and her eyes dwelt ever on him very steadfastly, and his on her, and neither took heed of Hunding, who watched them both. Eagerly she waited for him to tell them his name, expecting she knew not what; but as her eyes looked on him, she forgot even that Hunding had asked it, for she forgot all else except that in front of her and at her husband's table was seated the fair-haired stranger. As for him, his eyes were fixed in thought, as if he meditated on his answer. Yet since it was a strange thing that a guest should not tell his name to his host, again Hunding questioned him.

"Surely I would not press aught unwelcome on my guest," said he, "if he wills not to tell me. But see how my wife also waits for your answer. She too

would fain know the name of her guest
and mine;" and again he looked at
Sieglinde.

But she took not her eyes off the
stranger, for the sight of him fed her
heart, making her content. And though
she cared not to know his name, she
could not but do her husband's bidding,
and she too asked him his name, if so
be he would be willing to tell it.

Then again for a long moment was the
stranger still silent, but at the last he
raised his eyes and looked at her, and
some secret sympathy passed like a wave
between them; and he spoke to her
only.

"My name is Wehwalt, the man of
Woe," said he, "for mine is the portion
of sorrow, and my father was called 'The
Wolf.' He begat twins, a sister and

myself ; but while I was yet so young that
I scarce knew her name or the name of
my mother, the Wolf, my father, took me
into the forest, there to rear me up to
be strong and warlike, even as himself.
Strong too and warlike were his foes,
and there were many of them.   Then,
after years, one day he took me home,
but no home found we there, but only
the burnt ashes of what had been.   There
lay my mother, fallen and dead in defence
of the hearth, but of my sister no trace was
left.   Such was my home-coming."

He paused, but took not his eyes from
Sieglinde's face, and his voice rose in
sudden fire as he went on with his tale.

"The treacherous Niedings had done
this," he cried, "and deadly was their
work.   Bitter and relentless they pursued
us, and for years my father and I lived a

hunted life in the forest, beset with our foes. Yet ever his courage and his cunning avoided the snares they set for us, and, by the side of the Wolf, the Whelp grew up through boyhood to early manhood."

Thereat he paused again, and turned to Hunding.

"That Wolf's whelp tells you the tale," said he.

Now at the words of the stranger the suspicion that had hung over Hunding's heart like a poised hawk grew suddenly nearer, as if it stooped to its prey, for even in the manner in which the stranger told them his sister had been lost to him, in that manner was his own wife won. Well he remembered how the mother fought for the daughter, but at the end she was slain, and the house burnt, and the girl carried off by force ; and again the strange likeness of the two struck on his heart. As for his wife Sieglinde, her face was a mask, and she only gazed at the stranger with wide, grey eyes, and what she thought no man knew, and least of all her husband. Also he had heard stories of the Wolf and the Whelp, as the forest folk called them, and now the Whelp told the tale himself. But since he must needs know more yet, he curbed himself.

"Wehwalt," said he ; "Wehwalt, the Wolf's whelp, it is a strange story that thou tellest us. Of thy name in stories of strife and war I have heard men tell. Yet saw I never the Wolf thy father nor his son till to-day."

He would have said more, but Sieglinde, her eyes all aflame, interrupted him.

"Tell us the rest," she cried, and her voice strangled in her throat, for if Hunding remembered how his wife was carried off from the burnt home, should not she remember? "Tell us where thy father is to-day? Where is his home? Is it near—is it near?" she cried.

Then the stranger shook his head.

"Thou shalt hear," he said, "and I will tell thee all. For after the burning of the house, and the murder of my mother, and the seizing of my sister, ever more fiercely did the accursed Niedings press on us, for the blood, maybe, had whetted them. But the Wolf was ever stronger and more cunning than the men, and day after day he drove them through the forest, and in his paths the dead lay thick. Even as a ship scatters the spray in clouds before its bows, even so they fell off spent from his

advance, and he passed on over them,
I with him, heeding them as little, as
they writhed in their death agonies, as
the ship heeds the billows it ploughs
through. Thus fared we till the day
came when my father was not. A wolf-
skin I found in the forest, but of him no
trace. And whether he is dead I know
not, or whether," and his eye brightened
—"whether he was not of mortal birth,
and his work there was finished, and he
went whither he would."

For a moment he paused, and on one
side the eager grey eyes of the woman
met his, and by her sat her husband,
whose black eyes smouldered with hate
that was scarce concealed. But in the
light of the grey eyes he forgot the black.

"Wanting him," he said, " I left the
forest and lived among men and women

of civilized race. Yet wherever I went,
whether I sought for friend only, or sought
for wife, I prospered not, and he who
should have been friend turned from me,
and she whom I sought for wife thought
scorn of me, for ill-luck was ever about my
path. Did I think a thing right? That
was enough : to all others the deed seemed
foul. Did I think a deed false? To all
others it appeared fair. And thus I was
at war with the whole world. About my
path watched hate, and anger against me
grew like weeds in the bush. Did I seek
for joy? Bitterness was mine, and woe
and sorrow. Thus came I to call myself
Wehwalt, for woe was my fate. So I
named myself to fit my fate."

Then Hunding wiped his mouth, for he
had made an end of eating, and laughed
bitterly.

"Truly then thou hast named thyself," said he, "if none to whom thou goest as a guest is glad at thy coming, and slow to love thee, and grieves not when thou goest. And indeed such seems to be thy case."

At that Sieglinde turned and faced her husband, as she had never faced him before.

"Ah!" she cried, "there speaks the coward, Hunding. For who but a coward would insult a man who is alone, and who is weaponless?"

Then she turned to the stranger again.

"Guest of mine and of Hunding's," she said, "thy tale is but half told. How came it that thou art without thine arms? Where is thy shield and thy sword and thy spear, that thou goest at the mercy of every coward?"

At that Hunding laughed, for he was

minded to be amused. But she heeded not, and but listened for the stranger's words.

"It was thus that I lost my shield and spear and sword," said he ; "for I went to help and to rescue, if so be I could, a maid whom her kin wished to marry to a man she loved not. To me she came for help, and help I gave her, for I bethought me of how the Wolf would descend like a hill-top storm on to his foes, and I, his whelp, could do no other way. So hewed I and hacked among the cruel kin, for rage was in my heart, since it was by such unhallowed wooing that I had lost my sister, and I cleared the homestead of her evil clan. Two brothers had she, who would make the marriage, and for them I made a funeral instead of a marriage for their sister. But at that—ill-luck still following

me—the tenderness of the maid awoke,
and she wailed their loss, and her grief
conquered her erstwhile cry for help.
Thus for me who had delivered her she
had only curses.   Then, as I waited there,
rom every side swarmed out the kith and
the kin of those whom I had done to
death, so that the forest was thick with
them.   Yet the maid still bewailed her
brothers, and cursed me for their death,
and cursed herself for that she had bidden
me to aid her, and so compass it.   With
my sword I still defended her, for her kin
were thirsty for her blood, and with my
spear I sent more to their account, till at
the end my sword was shattered, and my
spear sundered.   Then with these eyes I
saw them murder the maiden as she still
bewailed her brethren ; and since I could
do no more, I fled from before their faces,

while she, dead, crowned the heaps of dead. So fled I, and came hither."

Then again he paused, and looked at Sieglinde with a pitiful entreaty.

"Thus is it with me," he said, "and thus it has always been with me. Am I not right then to name myself by a name of woe? Has peace or joy any lot with me?"

And the stranger got up, for he suddenly could bear her gaze no longer, and walked to the hearth. And she, when the magic of his gaze was withdrawn, turned pale suddenly, moved more deeply than she knew had been possible. Only Hunding still eyed him with growing hate and certainty. Already he knew enough, and his vengeance, so he swore to himself, should soon be complete. And he rose also and faced the stranger.

"Truly ill-luck has guided thee here,"

he said; "and ill-luck planted thy feet
when they came to the house of Hunding.
For have I not often heard of the race to
which thou belongest? And thou spakest
truly when thou saidst that thy coming
gave no joy to any host, for thou art of a
wild, unhallowed breed, whose right is
wrong in the eyes of all the world of men,
whose true is false, whose false is true.
All day have I been nearer to thee than
thou knewest of, and the adventure thou
hast told us is not yet complete."

With that he drew nearer to the
stranger.

" It is now my turn to tell my guest of
myself," he said, "and let him know where
my feet have borne me. It was kin of
mine whom thou hast slaughtered in im-
potent defence of a maid of my race; my
kin are the brothers you killed, and all

F

day I have been on the track of him who killed them. But all day have I been too late, though fast on the trail. Yet when I return home, whom find I at my hearth? Him, the murderer of my kin. Thus there is blood already between us, and ever shall be."

At his words his wife Sieglinde rose with terror and pity in her face, and drew near to the two men. But Hunding heeded her not.

" To-night," he said, " thou art guest of mine ; that must needs be so. But at dawn to-morrow, Wolf's whelp, I am thy host no more, and thou shalt answer for the blood of my kindred which thou hast shed. Hast thou no arms? So much the worse, for thou wouldest be safer for a sword, and at sunrise we meet. To-night we are host and guest, but a dawn

" To-night we are host and guest."

to-morrow be ready to meet me as the avenger of my kindred."

At these words Sieglinde could contain herself no more, but came quickly up, and placed herself between the two men.

" No, no!" she cried. " It cannot be, Hunding."

Then his wrath flamed up. " Hence, go hence," he cried; "get to thy work, and make ready my night-drink; go from the hall."

At his words she fell back, still pondering with her quick woman's wit as to how she could avert this. From the table she took the drinking-horn, and from the cupboard the spices with which she made the hot, fragrant draught which Hunding loved. And even as she turned to leave the hall, sudden and high like a summer fire in the forest her love for the stranger flamed in her heart, and with love a sudden wild up-springing of hope. He still stood by the hearth, scarcely heeding Hunding's words, for his eyes ever followed her, and as she was even now on the threshold, she cast one long glance at him, and then, as if leading his eye thither, looked to where the hilt of the sword in the ash-trunk glimmered in the firelight. Then she looked back to him, and knew that he understood not, for how should he understand?

But Hunding saw that she still lingered, and with furious finger pointed her forth, and she left them. Then he took his arms from the tree.

"Words for women, and weapons for men," said he. "Wolf's whelp, we meet to-morrow."

And he strode from the hall into his bed-chamber, leaving the stranger alone.

CHAPTER IV

THE RECOGNITION

So Hunding went forth and left the stranger alone with the leaping flames and shadows from the hearth. Long pondered he on what the day had brought forth, and what should be the burden of the morrow; but through all his thoughts there rose like a flame of dancing fire the thought of the woman Sieglinde, and of his love for her, and how he could help her to leave this house of hate. Weaponless was he, and her husband had mocked at him for it. Then his thoughts went backwards to the old wild days in the forest when he and his father, whom he had called by the name he was known to men, were the swift terror of their foes. And at that a sudden hope sprang up within him, for he remembered how his father had told him that when his need was sorest, a sword should be near him. Surely now his need was sore enough, yet where was the sword? At that he cried aloud on his father's name, the secret name known but to him, and "Walse, father Walse!" he cried, "show me the sword, for my need is sore."

No voice answered him, but the stillness was broken by the sound of the logs on the hearth suddenly falling together, and from the embers went up a sudden flame illuminating the walls, and gleaming on the sword-hilt. Then remembered he that Sieglinde's last look had directed his eyes there, but from where he sat he could see the gleam only, and knew not yet that it was a sword. Only he thought to himself that her last look had fallen there, and something of the gleam of her eyes still lingered there, making the dark stem bright. But the gleam was very steady, and he wondered at it.

Then the flames from the hearth grew low again, and the shadows thickened in the hall. But something of the brightness still lingered within him, and he thought of how the eyes of the woman had shone on him all the evening when they sat at meat, and it seemed to him as if his soul, on which long night had settled, had been bathed in the beams of morning. Light and hope she had brought to his darkened heart; for one day he had basked in sunshine, and ere yet his sun had sunk behind the hills again, one last evening ray had so

illumined the ash-stem, that something of
the light had still lingered there. Still
lingered it also in his heart, though she
had gone, and though the shadows of his
woes crowded fast upon him, even as upon
the walls of the dwelling-place they
gathered in growing battalions, as the
flames on the hearth sank ever lower. Yet
still he sat there with open unseeing eyes.
No thought of sleep was his. How could
he sleep when Sieglinde abode within the
house of hate? Round him the shadows
grew and thickened, and at length the last
sparks on the hearth were quenched, and
through the open chimney only there
filtered in a little greyness, so that though
all was dark, yet the density of that
blackness was greater here and less there.

How long he sat there, alert though lost
in reverie, he knew not, but at the end a

little noise fell on his ear and the door of
the bed-chamber was opened, and framed
in darkness he saw there a white figure.
And his heart so hammered within him,
that it seemed to him that the noise of it
must awaken Hunding. Yet he moved
not, neither spoke, and the figure came
nearer. Then a voice that he knew fell
like pearly rain on the stillness.

" Sleepest thou ? " she whispered.

Then he could stay still no longer, but
sprang up noiselessly.

" I ? " he stammered, " I sleep, when
thou seekest me ? "

" Listen," said she. " In Hunding's
night-draught I have mixed a sleeping
potion, and thus the whole night is before
us to devise a plan for thy safety."

" Safety ? " whispered he. " With thee
is my safety, and my——" And then, be-

cause he was Hunding's guest, he paused. Yet he was Hunding's foe at daybreak.

"But a sword, a sword!" she cried. "Ah! there is no need to speak low; we shall not waken Hunding, for I brewed his drink strong. Ah! could I but bring thee the sword, for a sword waits here for him who is fit to seize it. It is near to thee now, and truly thine is an hour of sore need."

"What sayest thou? What is it thou hast said?" cried the stranger.

So she told him the story of her marriage feast, of how another stranger had strode to the board, and flung the sword in the ash-stem.

"There, there," she said, pointing at it, looking where she had looked before; "and one, only one shall be able to move it. Ah! when he comes—he who is ordained—then shall my vengeance for the years of sorrow I have passed in the house of Hunding be sweet to my mouth. For every tear I have shed here, my mouth shall be full of laughter and joy ; for all the tears that I could not shed out of very bitterness and drought of soul, joy shall be mine too deep for smile or laughter. My friend, the friend of my soul, him I wait for, and with him there will be peace and victory for us both."

Then the stranger, knowing that there could be but one, and that his father whom he had called " The Wolf," who could cast a sword as the woman had said, and re-membering that he had told him that in the hour of his sorest need a sword should be near him, knew that this was the sword of which he spoke, and that it was he who should draw it forth. And knowing that,

he gave no more thought to it, for the
woman had said that he who should draw
it forth was the friend of her heart, and
that knowledge for the moment drowned
all else, and covered his soul with a huge,
soft billow of joy, so he gave no heed to
the sword, but only to her who stood by
him.   And in the exultation of his love he
laughed aloud, and passionately drew her
to him.

"And that is I, that is I!" he cried,
"O crown and flower of womanhood!
All my hopes in thee are fulfilled, and all
my failures in thee are mended.   Hard
and long has been the way that led us each
to the other.   Lo! I heal the wounds
which wrong has made, and thy hand
soothes and banishes all my woe.   Shame
has been thy portion in the house of hate.
Hunding thy husband!   No mumbling

vow hallows that unnatural union. Thou hast called for vengeance, and vengeance is at thy side, and the arm of vengeance thus wound round thee makes thee strong. But dearer and nearer I approach to thee than that. My hand bears vengeance for thee, but my heart bears love. Sieglinde! Sieglinde!"

Even as they stood thus, in the first transport of the knowledge that they loved, the great door of the hall swung open noiselessly, for maybe Hunding had not closed it when he returned home, and Sieglinde started in sudden alarm.

"What is that?" she cried. "Who went? Who has come?"

Slowly the door swung wide, and a great flood of moonlight poured in upon the pair, bathing them in its beams. High rose the moon in a cloudless heaven, and

the warm breeze of spring whispered
through the bushes and filled the hall.   At
length and at last the winter had ceased,
and spring, that moment of all the year
when the sap stirs in the trees, and the
birds are mated, and lion seeks lioness in
the Libyan hills, and man turns to woman
and woman to man, spring was upon them
in its overpowering fulness and sweetness.
None may resist its compulsion, nor did
they resist.   Gently he drew her to him,
and whether he spoke or sang she knew
not, or whether it was only the echo of her
thoughts she heard.   But it seemed to her
that his voice spoke.

" None went, but one has come," said he.
" Look you, this house is the house of hate
no longer, but the place of spring.   For
May has awoke, and the storms are hushed,
and winter is over, and the glory of spring

spreads round us. He wakes the warm winds, and as he wakes them they waft him on, and at his coming the wayside blossoms with its yearly miracle. Hedge and heath, field and forest are redolent with flowers, and as he moves across the world, laughter hails him on all sides. O! the time of the singing birds is come, and the breath of the earth is warm and sweet. Spring lies among the bushes, and where his warm body is pressed the flowers spring, and the young shoots of the trees, when they see his bosom rise and fall to the beat of his heart, put out their amorous branches to touch his fair form. Along the world strike his smiles, and with them, his sole weapons, he makes the whole world mad. The flash of his eye slays the winter, and at his glance the storms are hushed. All doors fly open to meet his coming, even as the door

G

of the house of hate opened just now of its own accord, and spring is here.

"And who walks with him? Love his sister. In our hearts she slept, and when he came the doors of our hearts were opened also, and she laughs when she sees the light. The walls that held us are crumbled, and she is free. Spring the brother meets love the sister, and they meet here on the threshold of our hearts. They have found each other, and we have found each other."

And whether she replied to him he knew not, or whether it was only the echo of his thoughts he heard, but it seemed to him that her voice spake.

"Spring," she said. "O spring, my brother, how have I sorrowed for thee and sought thee. Long has winter held us both, but when first I saw thee, how with love and I knew not what dread my heart was drawn to thee. Friendless was I, and he who was nearest to me was nearest also in hate. At length, at length thou camest, and at the first glance, I knew that thou wast mine, and all the secret treasure of my heart, all that I am, was poured out for thee. Friendless was I, and frost-bound of heart and utterly lonely. Then, O my friend, thou camest!"

And wonder and awe at the greatness and might of the gift that the spring had brought to both fell on them, and for a long while they stood thus content, if so be that lovers are ever content, in gazing at each other. Then the full love surged strong within them, so that speech could not be withheld, and Sieglinde wound her arms round his neck yet more closely.

"Let me gaze on thee," she whispered,

"for my senses reel with longing for thee, and reel in that they are satisfied when they behold thee. I am on fire."

"Yea, the moon makes thee on fire," said he, "and like living fire thy hair burns round thee. I gaze and I gaze, and still I am unfilled."

Then Sieglinde with her hand swept back the hair from his forehead, and with her finger, smiling like a child, she traced the path of the blood in his temple.

"See how thy life spreads like the boughs of a tree, and puts forth shoots in thy temples," said she. "I am faint and sick with content, yet even now sounds warning in my ears. Though never before have I seen thy face, yet long before have I known it."

"I, too," said he, "when dreams of love visited my sleep, have dreamed of thee and of no other. With what sadness did I behold thee then. And now, and now——"

"And often," said she, "as I gazed in the black lake, where it is still and waveless, have I seen thy face as in some magic mirror that showed me what should be. And now, and now——"

And like a child she laughed for pleasure, and as the wonder of their love grew and deepened, so the silence of love, more musical than hearing itself, descended on them. That long draught of silence was wine to each thirsty soul, and when they had drunk deep of it, again Sieglinde spake.

"Speak to me, and let me be silent listening," she said, "for thy voice comes to me out of the early years when I was but a child. Thy laugh rings to me out

of those golden mists before—before——"
and she shuddered at the thought of
Hunding.

"Speak thou," said he, "and let me
listen."

Again the tide of love filled her full,
even as the bitter creeks and marshes
are flushed with the return of the water.
Then struck her a sudden wild thought,
and again she gazed earnestly into his
eyes.

"Without words when thou came faint
with weariness, thy glance looked so to
me, till my despair was mild, and died
in the light of the day that streamed on
me. Wehwalt! ah no, such cannot be
thy name. What is there of woe left?
Not the shadow of the dream even!"

"No, I am Wehwalt no longer!" cried
he, "for thy love has banished woe from

me. That name which I gave myself is gone, for gone is woe. Ah, woman, woman, give me my name ; tell me by what name I shall be called, and that, thy gift, and none other shall be my name."

Then looked she at him as one half lost in thought.

" And Wolf, was Wolf thy father's true name ? " she asked.

" Wolf he was called," said the stranger, "and as Wolf he was feared, for he was as a wolf among timorous foxes. Yet it was not as Wolf I knew him. His glance was bright as thine, and as far-reaching, and that glance was the glance of Walse."

Then was that mystery of fate by which she was led to him, even as Spring the brother met Love the sister on the threshold of their hearts, made manifest to her, and the knowledge drove her beside herself.

" So," she said, " Walse was thy father, and thou art a Wolsung.   For thy sake did Walse fling the sword into the ash-stem, for well know I that it was Walse who flung it there and no other.   And on my tongue thy true name trembles, the name by which I love thee—Siegmund, Siegmund."

Then sprang Siegmund, stranger no longer, to the ash-stem, and in his right hand seized he the gleaming hilt.

" Thou sayest it ! " he cried, " and the sword shall prove I am Siegmund.   For Walse told me that when my need was sorest then should the sword of deliverance and victory be near me.   Has it not come ? Has not my need been sore ?   For love is the sorest need a man can know, and that is mine ; and deep is the dear wound it has made in my breast.   Burn deeper yet, O wound, stirring me to strife and strenuous

At that he wrenched
at the sword-hilt.

deed.   Lo! I name it, the sword of need—
Nothung, Nothung.   Come   forth   then,
Nothung, leave thy dark sheath, and bare
thy   shining   blade.   I, Siegmund, bid
thee."

And at that he wrenched at the sword-
hilt, and that which no power of the guests
of Hunding's marriage feast could stir,
moved at his bidding, and leaped forth to
his hand.   Bright and lordly shone it in
the moon of spring, and Sieglinde beheld,
and her eyes were dazzled with its shining,
even as her heart was dazzled with love.

Then cried Siegmund again : "Behold
me, Siegmund the Wolsung, the son of
Walse.   This is my bridal gift to thee, the
sword of victory and of thy deliverance.
Wife to me art thou by right, even as the
sword is mine by right.   Round thee
crumbles the house of hate.   Come forth,

come forth into the light of love.   Lo, the
house of hate and of spring opens its doors
wide, so follow, follow ! Nothung, thy
deliverance, and Siegmund, whose life is
thy love, go with thee."

He seized her with the violent tenderness
of love, and drew her to him.   Straight in
front of them opened the door into the
house of spring, and it was fair.   Yet, since
he knew not yet who it was he led out with
him, she spoke, even as he led her forth.

" Siegmund, Siegmund," she said, " O
take me, take me.   Thy longing has led
thee to me.   Is the flash of my eyes like
the flash in the eye of Walse thy father ?
So be it : for who else should be like
him but I ?   The burned homestead, the
vanished sister, dost thou forget them ?
By the sword, even as Walse said, thou
winnest her."

And for one moment Siegmund gazed at her in wild amaze. Then, for the spring was hot in his blood, and it was so written in the Book of Fate, to which even Wotan bows, whether he lords it in heaven, or as Walse he strides in the forest, there was no stop or stay for his passion.

" My bride, my sister ! " he said, " brother and bridegroom long for you. For the blood of the Wolsungs will blossom yet."

CHAPTER V

Not far from the house of Hunding, but above the great wood of pines that with their dark plumes fringed the hillside opposite, there was a region of wild and bleak rocks, where, if any breeze stirred below, here it was as a strong wind. And if storm was coming over the earth, here above all would the clouds gather, and gloom and mix together till the power of the heavens willed that they should go on their appointed journeys of wrath or mercy to the thirsty earth. Thus the Valkyries, the wild maidens of the storm,

were often wont to come here, riding on
the wings of the wind, for their joy was
in tempest and strife, and they cared little
for peace and content, and their home was
with the thunder, and the lightning was the
lantern they loved best. At other times,
when the heavens were clear, and the
benediction of the sun brooded over the
earth, here, above the woods and the
damp and sorry lowlands, was its light the
most serene and bright. Pure blew the
airs as they blew to the mariner in the
shrouds of his ship, and on all sides carved
out to infinite distance lay vales and
mountain peaks and ridges of hills, folded
and knit the one into the other as the
muscles of a strong man's arm rise and fall
into ridge and furrow where his strength
abides.

Thus it was that Wotan the king of

the gods often came here, for here it was
that he would be like to find his daughter
Brunnhilde, the eldest of the Valkyries, and
of all living things the dearest to him ; and
from here, as from a fortress home, she and
her sisters, having communed with their
father, would start on their war-raids, riding
on the storm, and dazzling the souls of men
with their beauty and their terror.   And on
the selfsame night, that first of spring, when
spring and love awoke together in the
hearts of Sieglinde and Siegmund, and
maddened them with their sweetness, Wotan
with his daughter Brunnhilde had sat
night-long on that serene mountain-top, and
he, communing with her as he communed
with his own soul, had spoken to her of that
wild deed which the brother and sister, his
children by the forest maiden, had committed.   And in the deeps of his heart

he guessed, though darkly as in a glass, that from Siegmund the Wolsung should come that man for whom he waited, one free and owing nothing to the favour of the gods, who alone should be able to bring back to him the ring of the Rhine-gold, in whose circlet lay the wealth of the world and unmeasured might, even as Erda had foretold to him. Nor did the mating of this strange pair amaze or disquiet him, for they loved with that love which is the fire of the earth, and without which the earth would grow cold, and to his eyes that fire, from whatever fuel it was kindled, was a thing sacred beyond compare ; while of the vows of a loveless marriage, such as Sieglinde's had been, he recked nought, nor scrupled to scatter it to the winds, even as a man on an autumn day scatters the thistledown on the breezy uplands,

H

and cares nought where the winds may
take it.   For as light as thistledown to him
were loveless vows, but love, even though
no vow may hallow it, he held more sacred
than his own oath.

So when the day dawned, he rose from
the rock where he had been sitting, and
Brunnhilde rose from her place by his knee.

" Up then to horse, my maid, " he cried,
"and be strong and swift to aid. Ere long
the clash of arms shall be heard, and
Hunding follow hard on Siegmund's trail.
Up then, Brunnhilde, and put might into
the heart of Siegmund the Wolsung, and
strength into his arm.   I reck nothing of
Hunding, for he is no son of light, but of
darkness.   So to horse and away ; get thee
to Siegmund's side."

Then loud and long Brunnhilde shouted
her cry of war, so that the rocks re-echoed,

and far away from the muffled hillside of pines came the response.

Then ere she went, she climbed quickly to the topmost pinnacle of the ridge of rocks, and looking down into the ravine behind, she saw one whom she knew coming quickly up, and with a sweet sort of malice in her heart she called to her father Wotan.

"Fly, father, fly!" she cried, half laughter, half pity for him. "Let the king of gods be seen to fly for his safety, for a storm for thyself sweeps hither swiftly. Fricka thy wife is near on thy trail, driving her chariot with its harnessed rams. Up the path she comes ; canst thou not hear the strokes of her golden whip, which like a flail she is plying ? Listen to the bleatings of her belaboured steeds, listen to the rattling of her whirling wheels, while to

guide her path to thee, anger flares like a
beacon in her face.   Father, dear father,
such fights as these are little to my liking,
for   Brunnhilde   would   sooner   meet   the
armed strength of men than the spirted
venom of a woman's tongue and her war
of words.   Meet thou this fight as thou
best may, for in such case I love to desert
thee, and laughing I desert thee now.
Yet I will wait hard by till Fricka has gone,
and once more talk with thee ere I go to
aid Siegmund."

Then once again, turning a look of love
and laughter on her father, Brunnhilde
shouted her joyous war-cry so that the
distant hills replied, and sped quickly away
until Fricka should have done with Wotan.
With love shining in his eyes for her, he
saw her go, and with anger and misgiving
in his heart he saw his wife approach,

knowing that a war of words was before
him. For well he knew that she had come
on this selfsame matter of Siegmund and
Sieglinde, for so lawless a deed was an
outrage to her. Yet was Wotan's purpose
undismayed, and he swore to himself that
she should find him steadfast in his resolve
to aid Siegmund.

Now Fricka, though she was Wotan's
wife, was not the companion of his heart ;
for she was cold and hard of nature,
and nought that was human beat in her
bosom. And by the great human heart of
Wotan, in whose nostrils love was the
breath of life, this wife of his was honoured
indeed and much feared, but it was not to
her he whispered at dark, nor told the
secret troubles and joys of his soul. And
when he saw her driving down the path,

though he marvelled at her beauty, he had no word of tender welcome for her, and indeed her face was one flame of anger.

"Here in these heights where thou hidest from me, thy wife," she said, "I seek and find thee. Give me thy oath that thou wilt help me."

Then said Wotan, "What ails thee, wife?"

"Hunding's cry for vengeance has come to my ears," said she. "And well it might, for, as thou knowest, I am the goddess of marriage and marriage vows. Thus I listened in horror and holy indignation to the tale I heard, and I have sworn that Siegmund and Sieglinde, who have thus put him to shame so foully and madly, should pay for their sin. So help me, swear that thou wilt help me, that the two may reap their right reward. For shameful and impious is the deed that has been done."

Even as she spoke a little red flower blossomed at Wotan's feet, opening suddenly at the dawn of this sweet spring morning, and above his head two birds mated in mid-air, and his heart was warm within him with the instinct of the spring-time. " It is the spell of the spring," he thought to himself. " Love and spring drove mad both man and woman, and if there is blame, the blame is there. " Aloud he said—

" O Fricka, it is spring-time ! " and almost a tear of tenderness for the frail race of men he so loved started to his eye.

But Fricka answered him in anger. " The marriage vow has been broken," she cried, " and though that is not all, yet that is enough. Hunding's house is dishonoured, and I hate those who have dishonoured it."

"And did love hallow that marriage vow?" cried Wotan. "Was not Sieglinde carried by force to her marriage feast? Love's hand signed not the bond, and where love is not, there the most solemn vow turns impious. But a stranger came, and love stirred at last for him and her. And where love stirs, there is true marriage, and those stirrings of love I abet, I approve."

"Be it so," said Fricka; "let us say that the loveless wedlock is unholy, that it is best honoured when broken. But that is not all, and thou knowest it. For is it holy that two twins should seek each other thus? Ah! Wotan, my head reels and my senses are bewildered when I think of that. Brother and sister? When has it happened that a man should marry his neighbour in his mother's womb? When has that happened?"

But Wotan looked at her gently.

"It has happened now," he said. "Wife, is there nought left for us to learn? Thou knowest, thou knowest well that between the two there burns the authentic fire of love. It has happened. Siegmund and Sieglinde have so loved. Therefore, as I do, bless their union and blame it not. It is spring-time too."

Then was Fricka's wrath so kindled that it seemed as if she had been calm before and was now angry for the first time, and with storm she descended on him.

"Then is our godhead perished!" she cried, "since thou didst beget thy godless Wolsungs. Do you think that I shall follow thee on such a road? For the stones of it are shame, and shameful is the foot that treads thereon.   Hunding's cry goes up unanswered, and all that was holy thou tramplest on.   All this because the twins that thou begottest, in unfaithfulness to me thy wife, have dared to do this impious deed.   Vows! what are vows to thee?   Thou holdest none sacred.   I have ever been true to thee, and ever thou hast betrayed my truth.   There is no mountain top that has not seen, no vale that has not concealed some pleasure of thine, pleasure that scorned and dishonoured my faithfulness.   When thou wentest to Erda, and begottest the brood of Valkyries, Brunnhilde the first, I bore it, for Erda was ever noble, and such adventure was not altogether base.   But now like a common man thou goest on thy foul adventures, haunting the forest till men call thee the Wolf, or passing under the name of Walse. There is no plumb-line to measure the depths of thy shame, so deep is that abyss. These hast thou begotten of a mere woman, a she-wolf, these twins. And now thou flingest me at the feet of thy she-wolf's litter. Ah, mete out the full measure of my shame. Thou hast betrayed me, and now thou stampest me beneath thy feet and the feet of thy children of shame."

Wotan answered her not at once, for indeed there is no use in answering an angry woman, and he knew well that there were certain things that Fricka would never know. For her mind moved not from that little circle in which it was wont to go round, and all that had not happened, but which was still among the unfound things of the world, was outside her understanding.   But Wotan knew that all heaven and earth was waiting for a hero who should come, who should make the old things new, and repair that which was outworn. He should be one who was utterly free, not sheltered or befriended by the gods, and not serving their laws.   Nor might the gods help in this work, for their work was of an earlier day, and he who should come must pass beyond them both in thought and deed.   Yet as Fricka still said nothing, but stood with heaving bosom, he spoke of him who should come whom he knew, though darkly, should be of the wild Wolsungs. Yet he knew also she would understand not. Nor did she understand, but answered him according to her own sightlessness, saying that since all that was done on earth was the work of men, whose life lay in the hands of the gods, what was there a man could do which was forbidden to the gods?

" For who," cried she, "put might into men except thou, or who but thou put courage into their hearts, and strength into their arms? Thou only. Yet now thou sayest that one will come of thy Wolsung breed who is outside and beyond. Dost then think to trick me thus? Surely I know that he, like all other men, must be subservient to thy will. It is to shield thy shameful twins that thou sayest this. It is by thy will alone he walks."

" Not so," said Wotan ; " for when Siegmund seized the sword, he did it of his own might. In nought did I help him there. By the might of that sword he walks alone, not upheld by my power."

Then Fricka, for in her woman's way she was cunning, saw her path.

"Then shield him no further," she said quietly, "and take back thy sword, the sword that thou hast given him."

"How can I?" said he. "For Siegmund won it for himself in his need, and Siegmund's it is."

"But from thee," said she, "came not only the sword, but the need. In those days, when thou didst fling the sword at the ash-stem, I followed hard on thee, and saw thy deed. Who flung it there? Thou, Wotan. Who led Siegmund's hand to the hilt? Who but thou? Thou knewest where the sword was; in the presence of Sieglinde thou didst place it there. From thee, through her, the knowledge of it came to him. How canst thou say then that this Siegmund of thine is the hero that should come, since it is through thee he works?"

Then was Wotan both wroth and sorry, for he knew that Fricka spoke truth, yet he would have shielded Siegmund from her wrath. And she, seeing that she shook his will, spoke freely and calmly.

"Lo, the master does not war with slaves," she said, "nor fight for them. But thou and I, Wotan, are gods and equal. And I, whose soul and body are yet at thy bidding, wilt thou shame me and the vows I uphold before a mere man? Shall I be a laughter to the scornful, and shall men make merry over my downfall in their homes? Thou wilt not have it so; I know thou wilt not. My godhead is more to thee than that."

"What wilt thou then?" said he.

"That thou stand aside from the Wolsung."

Then Wotan was sore distressed and

very heavy at heart. "Let him go," said he, and his voice was low and troubled; "I will not stay him, nor shalt thou."

"Then shield him not nor shelter him," said she, "when vengeance follows on him."

Then did Wotan remember that he had bidden Brunnhilde to aid him, and it was ill to fight against Brunnhilde. Thus perhaps might Siegmund be safe. So he swore to Fricka that he would not shield nor shelter him. Yet Fricka was not yet satisfied.

"Look in my face, Wotan," she said. "Thou sayest thou wilt not shield him, neither shall thine shield him. No aid must he obtain from thy Valkyrie maidens."

"The Valkyries go where they will," said he, "and I have no power over them."

"So that was thy thought!" said Fricka. "It shall not be so. Thy will directs them; let it direct them that they turn not to Siegmund."

Then Wotan clenched his hands together, for this way and that was he torn. On the one side stood Siegmund his son, whom he must needs aid for the sake of the promise he had given with the sword; on the other, Fricka his wife. And in his agony he cried aloud—

"How can I slay him? It was he who found my sword."

"Let it be to him only a sword then," said Fricka, "and not the sword of Wotan, or break it in his hand, so that Hunding has him defenceless. O, Wotan," and as she spoke he knew in his heart her nobility and uprightness, for all that she was cold and hard, "O, Wotan, thou lovest me not, and I know it, yet shield my honour for never have I brought dishonour on thine. I ever upheld the marriage vow, and how would the sons of men laugh, and how would the glory of the gods be diminished, should thy daughter Brunnhilde not uphold it this day. How would lawlessness and unhallowed lust be master among men. By Siegmund's death alone is my honour upheld, for he has sinned against me. So swear to it, Wotan."

Even as she spoke Wotan heard again the joyful war-cry of Brunnhilde, who, supposing that his strife with Fricka was over, was coming nigh to where they stood, and he remembered in his heart how so short time ago he had bade her warn and shelter Siegmund. Yet he could in nought gainsay his wife, and in sorrow and heaviness he cast himself down on the

*" I give thee mine
ath ! " said he.*

rocky seat where he had sat with his maiden. And his voice came hollow and broken, like an echo buffeted against rocks.

" I give thee mine oath!" said he.

Then having the oath of Wotan which he might not break, Fricka turned at once from him, for she had accomplished her purpose, and went where she had left her chariot drawn by rams. Near by was Brunnhilde standing with her horse, and as she passed her—

" Thy father waits for thee," she said. " Go thee and learn from him that which he has chosen." Then mounting her chariot, she lashed the rams with her golden whip, and they sped down the mountain-side.

CHAPTER VI

SIEGMUND'S LOT IS CAST

BUT Brunnhilde had heard Fricka laugh as she mounted her chariot, the which boded no good thing to her father Wotan; and as she approached him she saw that he leaned his head on his hand in great heaviness, and was as one utterly cast down.

"Father, father, what is it?" she said. "What sorrow holds thee? Never have I seen thee so."

Then Wotan's arm dropped, and his head sank on his bosom. "I am bound by the fetters I have forged," said he.

"All are free but I, the lord of all.   O
shame, O bitter ill-hap, and worm that
dies not.   There is no sorrow so heavy as
mine!"

Then did Brunnhilde drop her spear and
helmet in sudden alarm and forgetfulness,
and in the hope to soothe and comfort him,
for never had she seen him so.   She laid
loving hands upon his knees, and sat
herself at his feet, and asked him tenderly
to tell her what had befallen, for his look
frightened and amazed her.   So she
besought him to tell her all, for she was
ever true to him, and ever had he trusted
her.   Then by slow degrees Wotan aroused
himself, and laid a hand on her bright hair,
which he caressed lovingly.   But when he
spoke his voice seemed to come from afar,
for his mind had been brooding on that
which had been long ago, and on that

which time to come should bring out of
what had been, for out of the womb of the
past is born what shall be.   And dim and
dark was his voice, even as that on which
he thought had been dim and dark, and he
spoke slowly and with many pauses, of
days long dead, and of days yet far off, the
heirs of ages not yet born.   But through-
out he looked earnestly into Brunnhilde's
eyes, for she was his most own, and when
he looked there, he saw himself and his
own will and purpose.

"In days of old," said he, "when the
first heat of youth was passed, I set myself
to win the world, and all craft in bargains
was mine, and, so that I worked my will,
I stooped to any falsehood.   Yet never
for long could I withhold myself from
love, and its sweetness ever allured my
senses and my might.   But Alberich, that

son of night, who inhabits the dark places
of the earth, had forsworn all love, and
since he never yielded to it, but cursed
it, he won for himself the secret treasure
of the gold which abode in mid-Rhine,
and by its might, for it is the world's
wealth, reached his hands about the world.
Yet by guile I got it from him, and with
it I paid the giants who built me the walls
of Walhalla that are a rein and a bridle
to the world. Then once again was I
safe. Yet Erda gave me words of
warning about the ring, and told me
that Walhalla itself would fall, yet could
tell me nought fully, till with the spell
of love upon her she spake. Yet that
selfsame spell of love between her and
me gave me thyself, Brunnhilde, and thy
eight sisters of the storm. With you I
thought to make Walhalla safe, and I

bade you slay and bring to be its guardians and the protection of its walls heroes and men of might, who should guard it well. Eternal life I breathed into them, and a mighty host uprose."

Then Brunnhilde smiled at him.

"And have we not done thy bidding?" she asked. "What cause for sadness is here? For the defenders of Walhalla are many in multitude: all these we have brought thee, as thou didst bid us."

Then spake Wotan again, his eyes dwelling ever on Brunnhilde.

"Moved by that spell of love, Erda told me where fear was. It is from Alberich the end will come to the gods, their evening, their dusk, if once again he gets the ring. While he has it not, I fear not him nor the hosts of night that he brings with him, for well Walhalla is guarded by heroes. But in pay for the building of Walhalla I gave it to the giant Fafner, who guards it ever and since I gave it him, I may not take it from him, for the bargain I made with him forbids me. Nor must he who shall take it from him owe ought to me ; he must be a free man, who for his own need, and without help trom me, shall wrest it from Fafner. Ah, where to find him ? How direct his course, yet without aiding or protecting him ? His might unaided must accomplish my wish. Wherever I work, there see I the fruits of my work, that which my hands have made. But he who shall take the treasure from Fafner must be free, unfettered, no slave or creation of mine."

Then Brunnhilde started up, for she saw what was in Wotan's mind.

"It is he then, Siegmund the Wolsung, who shall do this thing!" she cried. "Ever has he been unblessed and unhallowed of the gods."

But Wotan shook his head.

"So thought I," said he, "and with that thought in my heart, I reared him ever to work against the gods, so that he owed nought to us. Nothing has he but the sword he himself found. Yet, that was mine. It was I who gave him both sword and the need by which he found it. Scornfully Fricka unfolded that to me, piercing my soul to its uttermost. And thus I must serve her will."

Then wild amaze seized hold on Brunnhilde.

"Then dost thou forsake Siegmund?" she cried.

At that a wild tumult of rage and

despair seized on the god, for the words of Erda, which she had told him, grew clear to him.

"The curse is fallen on me," he cried; "and though I flee from it, it still follows me. For when I stole the ring of the Rhine-gold from Alberich, he said that what I loved I must needs forsake, and that him whom I trusted I must do to death. Even so it is. Behold the dusk deepens round me, and I hope for one thing only, the end. And on the end thinks Alberich, for the wild words of Erda, which never till now did I fathom, grow clear to me. For she said that when the dark enemy of love begets a son, then too is begotten the fall of the gods. And this too has happened, for Alberich has lovelessly bought a woman's undoing, and already the weeks of her deliverance are numbered, and the child waxes in her womb. Yet I for all my wooing could never beget that which I need, that free man of whom I spake. Oh! my bitterest blessing on thy work, Alberich; already I grow wan with the approaching end; already my godhead is but a tawdry mask. Bare thy fangs then: let thy hate and thy hunger make meat of me!"

The words died on his lips, and despair like a wave overwhelmed him. Then Brunnhilde nestled yet nearer to him, and the child-instinct within her spake, if so be she might comfort him.

"Father, father," she said, "what can thy child do?"

Then Wotan laughed bitterly.

"Fight Fricka's battles," said he, "and range thyself with her marriage vows and plighted troths. Siegmund is not the free man my soul longs for. So range thyself with Fricka's champion, the noble Hunding. Even so: death is decreed for Siegmund; be swift and brave to compass that. Thou wilt need all thy boldness, my child, for he is no coward whom Walse taught in the woods, and swift is his sword. Nor wilt thou find a foeman who fears thee; his eye will flinch not, though he beholds thee in all thy strength and terror."

Scarcely then could Brunnhilde believe what she seemed to hear, for she knew that her father loved Siegmund, and that the Wolsung was dear to his soul. Ever had he taught her to love him, for Siegmund was dauntless of heart, and knew not what fear was.

"It cannot be," she cried, "never can I lift my arm against him!"

Then Wotan rose in wrath, for it was as if his will disobeyed him when Brunnhilde was rebel, for indeed the maid was none other than his will.

"Thou darest? Thou darest?" he cried. "And does fear not look in thine eyes at the thought of disobedience? Am I a mock to thee? Indeed there will be for thee an end of mocking if thou rousest my wrath. For there is woe to any with whom Wotan is wrath, for I walk with the thunder at my call, and my hand holds and steers the lightning. Think thou of that, and give good heed. Thou knowest my will; see that thou performest it. Siegmund is numbered with the dead, and by Brunnhilde's hand shall that numbering be accomplished."

And he stormed forth in fury, the light-

Very slowly she
armed herself.

ning flickering about his path, and left Brunnhilde there.

Never before had he gone from her in anger, and she sat long where he had left her, wondering what this should mean, and what the day should bring forth. Oftentimes in hour of war had she seen him girt about with fury, but now it was she whom his rage threatened. Then she stooped down, and picked up again her spear and helmet and shield which she had laid on the ground when she spake with Wotan, and very slowly, with the joy of war altogether gone from her heart, she armed herself. For indeed her heart was not in this fight, and she went out to it with no joyful war-cry as was her wont. For the battle was against her friend, whom Wotan had ever taught her to love, and the wild Wolsung Siegmund had all her life been dear to her. Yet must Wotan's hest be obeyed.

So she turned and would have gone on her joyless errand, when suddenly she was aware that two were approaching up the rocky height; and as they came more nigh she saw they were none other than Siegmund and Sieglinde. Then pity so seized on her that she was but as wax, and, lest her will should fail utterly, she turned again quickly and went to the cavern hard by where she had tethered her horse on the coming of Fricka. Heavily she went to him, for the work before her was bitter and grievous to her.

CHAPTER VII

THE FIGHT OF SIEGMUND

SWIFTLY came Sieglinde up the rocky
path, and Siegmund followed hard after
her, bidding her rest and not fare so wildly
on ; for after that the spell of spring and of
love had so wrought within her that she
recked nothing of leaving the house and
hearth of Hunding, and the transport and
sweet madness of her love had been fulfilled, horror and dread had seized the
woman's heart, and she was distraught
with unspeakable dismay at her wild
adventure. Then had she risen up from

his side in the middle of the spring night, even while he, filled full of love, was sleeping, to escape from what she had done. But at her stirring he had awoke, and through the hours betwixt that and day had he followed after her, she still flying from him through field and forest. For at first on that evening of yesterday, which in the morning's light seemed to her so long ago, the torrent of her love had carried her unthinking, but now it seemed to her that her deed was altogether unholy. Utterly had she loved the man, and utterly was his love hers, and so great was the might of that and the transport of its power, that in its first outpouring it seemed to her that all else was of no import beside it. But afterwards she had thought on what she had done, and shame and horror burned within her with as

fierce a flame. Loveless had her marriage
with Hunding been, yet marriage it was,
and hallowed by the ordinance of the
gods. But this was lawlessness incar-
nate, and unnatural wedlock. Yet in her
woman's heart she blamed Siegmund not
at all; the blame in her mind was wholly
hers. She had brought shame on herself,
but that was a small thing compared to
the shame in which she had made him a
partaker.

But now for very weariness her limbs
could bear her no further, and at the top
of the rocky path nigh to where Wotan
and Brunnhilde had sat that night, she
faltered, and it was his arm that saved her
from falling.

"Wait, wait," he whispered. " Speak to
me, and let us have done with this dumb-
ness of fear. Thou art safe; my arm

encompasseth thee ; there is no fear while thou leanest on my breast."

At his touch, again the eternal woman of her nature awoke, and as he led her very gently to the very seat where Wotan had sat with Brunnhilde by his knee, she clung passionately to him, and gazing long into his face, embraced him. Yet even while her lips met his, the horrors of the night rose insurgent within her, and again she flung herself off from him, shame branding her, as a felon is branded.

"Siegmund, Siegmund!" she cried. "What have we done? Shame on me, shame on me!"

"Shame there has been, Sieglinde," said he, "and that when thou didst abide in the house of Hunding. But that shame shall I soon wash away with his blood, and in that crimson stream shall it be cleansed. Ah, fare not on so wildly; wait here, for I am well assured that he will come here in pursuit, and here also shall he meet the fate which has been appointed by him who in my sorest need granted me to find the sword. O sword of my need," cried he, and his fingers tightened on its hilt, "not in vain have I called on the name of vengeance. Surely I will repay."

Then was she a little quieted at his loving touch, and at the fierceness of surety of his hate towards Hunding, but soon she started up and listened.

"Horns, I hear horns!" she cried, "and the shouts of the pursuers. The shouts of the pursuers sound ever nearer, and strike the sky and echo from the hills. Hunding has woke from his night-draught, and is hot of foot on the trail.

He calls on his kindred to help him, and loosens the hounds of hunting. They nose thy trail, and thirstily they give voice, and their thirst waits to be assuaged by blood."

Loudly and in panic terror she cried, but at the end her voice failed, and her arm outflung dropped nerveless, and over her weary eyes drooped the shelter of her eyelids.

"Siegmund, where art thou?" she murmured. "Where art thou? I search for thy look; oh, let it light on me again; leave me not, Siegmund, oh, leave me not. Hark, hark! again I hear that deep baying of the hounds of death; they thirst for thy blood, and their fangs white and sharp grow red with the meat of their hunting. They reck not of thy sword, so fling it away. Hide, let us hide where none shall find us. Thy sword is shattered ; what toy-thing is this ?—thou fallest reeling. . . . Siegmund . . . . Siegmund . . . ."

At that her head drooped and she sank like a thing broken in his arms. It was in vain that he tried to rouse her, and only by the rise and fall of her bosom did he know she lived. So very gently—for, after the labour and travel of the night, it might be that she would sleep—he laid her back on the ground, and made for her a pillow of his knee, to rest her head. But she moved not, nor opened her eyes, yet, for her bosom still rose gently and fell, he comforted himself, and bending over her kissed her on the forehead. Thus they sat, and he grieved over her.

But by now had Brunnhilde put bridle again on to her horse Grane, and led him lightly out of the cavern, and came upon Siegmund and his bride sitting thus. And he was aware of her coming, and looked up, and saw her glorious face ; but there was no smile there, for the work before her gave no joy to her. Gravely she looked at him, and her heart was stirred with sorrow for the deed that her father had laid on her to do, and her eyes burned large with doom.

"Siegmund, I am here," she said, "and from here soon I lead thee. Thou seest that I am near thee ? "

And Siegmund answered : "Yes, but I know thee not," and a strange cold heaviness was lead in his limbs and in his eye.

"I come near to those whom death comes near to," said she, "and none others see me. He into whose eyes I

look stays not in the light.   With me
thou goest, and thou goest with me
far."

Then something of the great calm with
which death is ever girt about, struck
on Siegmund's heart, but he was not
afraid.

" And where goest thou ? " he asked.

" I go to Walhalla," said she, "where
the great father waits thee.   There lovingly will the hands of dead heroes greet
thee ; with hands outstretched and with
smile of welcome will they greet thee."

" And shall I find there Walse, the
Wolsung's father ? " said he in wonder.

" His face too shall greet thee."

" And will there be a woman there too,
to greet me ? " asked he.

" Yea, surely," said she.   " The maidens
of his will are there, and she who will

hand thee the gladsome wine is Wotan's daughter. Red is that wine, and with it are the hearts of heroes made glad."

But it was not after Wotan's daughter that Siegmund asked, and again he said:

"O most holy and austere of maidens, Wotan's child, truth is written in thine eyes, and truth thou wilt tell me. It is not of such I ask, but of my bride Sieg-linde. Will she be there?"

But Brunnhilde shook her head.

"Death comes not for her yet," she said, "and she shall not be there."

Then Siegmund laughed.

"Then get thee back to Walhalla," cried he, "and give my greeting to the high walls of Wotan, and to him who sits therein and is lord thereof. And greet for me Walse"—for he knew not that Walse his father was none other than Wotan—

"and greet the many heroes and the maidens of the will of the highest. But I come not after thee."

Then Brunnhilde was very sorry, yet what was to be, was to be.

" Siegmund," she said, " thou hast looked on me, and with me thou must go. Lightly thou reckest of mortal foes, for thy limbs are strong, but the wise man wars not against death. I am here to claim thee for him."

But though a chill seemed to fall round Siegmund, as if the sun had passed behind a cloud, yet was he not afraid; and, lo! his dear burden still leaned at his knee.

" I come not," he said, " for where Sieglinde is, in weal or woe, there I abide, and go not thence. Thy face daunts me not, I shrink not before thy glance, though bright it is with the brightness of danger.

Besides, who is it that deals death to me?"

"The hand of Hunding," she said. "For thus—at last—the lot was cast."

But Siegmund only smiled, and his fingers dwelt lovingly on the sword-hilt.

"I fear not that," he said, "for it is by my hand that he will fall, and if thou seekest a dead man, I will give thee a corpse, but not mine. Look at my sword, for he who let me gain it, promised my safety. Thus thy threats and thy warning are idle words, the buzzing of a fly."

Then Brunnhilde's face grew stern and set.

"He who let thee gain the sword," she cried in a loud voice, "now is determined otherwise, and has decreed thy death. Thus the magic of the sword is a thing of nought, a shadow that has passed away."

But at her raised voice, Siegmund forgot death and the sword and all else, and feared only that she would wake Sieglinde, who now slept gently.

" Be still, be still," he whispered, "and wake her not."

And he bent over her, and sorrowed for her, for it seemed to him that all the world was gathered against her whom he loved so well, and that he alone, for whom she had braved the wrath of men and gods, was on her side. Should then he forsake her? And if, as the maid had told him, the giver of the sword was now unfaithful, and decreed him death, then he would have none of his Walhalla ; Hella were sweeter to his troubled soul. High burned his anger at this unfaithfulness, and he turned to the maid who stood watching him.

" If then death is decreed for me," he

L

said, "think you I will be at ease in Walhalla? Nay, Hella rather than such peace."

Then Brunnhilde's stern glance softened, and she marvelled that he so loved the woman.

"Then is eternal joy so worthless to thee?" she asked him softly. "Dost thou desire nothing but the woman who is sleeping there? Is nought else sweet to thy soul, and nought else desirable?"

And he looked at her with bitterness, and marked the softened glance of her eye. Yet though she appeared so young and so maidenly, her heart must needs be utterly cold, since she did not comprehend how a woman filled the heart of the man who loved her.

"Dost thou mock me?" he said. "For what else could I care than that which lies

here ? I think thou art a foe to me, and
would gladly see harm and woe come to
me. Be it so ; and may my grief satisfy
the greed and hunger of thy heart. But
as for Walhalla—it is idle for thee to name
it to me. Dost thou not see ? Here is my
heaven and my rest."

Then she began to understand the need
of his heart, and with that she felt a tenderness for both him and the woman which
was new to her.

"Yes, yes," she said, " I feel what thou
feelest. But, Siegmund, what must be,
must be. Leave her then to me. Safely
and surely will I ward her and keep all
harm from her."

And she would have lifted Sieglinde up
and taken her to some hiding-place of
safety, but he stopped her.

"Stay," said he, "she is mine, mine, and

no other shall touch her. If so be that I must die, as thou sayest, it is better, it is better—for all the whole world is against her—that she should die, here, now. I will slay her myself as she sleeps, and death will come softly to her as a dream. Thus she will be at peace."

Then did the tumult and trouble in Brunnhilde's heart seethe and stir.

"No, no!" she cried. "Listen to me, for thou speakest wild words. The sacred pledge of love which thou hast given, for that I plead. Siegmund, Siegmund, thou canst not slay thy son!"

Yet he drew the sword, and brandished it.

"His is the blame," he cried, "who promised me victory with this sword, who now turns his back on me, faithless and untrue. Yet shall it aid me, for that with it I can give peace to her. Strike then, sword of need, sever both lives at once."

But at the sight of his sword uplifted to strike, all the woman in Brunnhilde rose invincible, and the solemn command of Wotan that she should fight for Hunding weighed lighter than chaff. In a moment her mind was made, and counting not the cost, she knew that she must needs befriend Siegmund and fight for him, and the thunders and terrors of Wotan had no weight with her. And with a cry she stayed his arm.

"Ah, I break," she cried. "I cannot do the deed that was laid on me. She shall live, she shall live, and instead of death I will bring thee the joy of victory. No longer fight I for Hunding; it is thee, Siegmund, whom my shield will shelter. So up, up; already the horns of battle sound nearer. What shall be, I cannot tell, but the sword thou wieldest is good steel, and the shield of me, Brunnhilde, will guard thee in the coming fight. Hail to thee, Siegmund, hail! At the fight I await thee."

All her face was afire with human love and pity, and so great a change was there from the look of that stern cold maiden and her pitiless beauty, that Siegmund could scarce believe that this was the same Brunnhilde. But at her words, joy and gladness uplifted him, and his heart, erstwhile full of despair and bitterness, was once more strong and hopeful. But Brunnhilde tarried not, for indeed, as she said, the horns of battle sounded near, but swung herself on to her horse, and rode swiftly off among the rocks towards the horns and approaching battle, and the noise of her horse's hoofs sounded fainter, and then was silent.

Now as they thus spoke together, behold the heavens had grown very black, and over the bright aspect of the sky had ridden swiftly up the storm-rack, low and sullen-looking, and torn into streamers and ribands of wrath. Already the hills and vales beyond had been entirely blotted out, and by now the clouds had reached even to that rocky ridge not far from where Siegmund sat, while mingled with the trouble and menace of the heavens came the blast of the horns of battle sounding ever nearer, and Siegmund knew that it was time for him to be gone to meet the black foe who awaited him. Then very gently he got up, and without waking Sieglinde, laid her back against the rocky seat, and once more bent over her, to see how she fared. The blessed balm of sleep had been spread over her eyes, and she was at rest, and her heart was unconscious of the wild alarms of war. And Siegmund wondered whether it was the maiden, who seemed so fierce and cold, but whose soul at the end had been touched with so gentle and womanly a pity, who had shed this gift on the woman, thinking that the clash of swords and the din of battle would daunt her. Then even as he bent over her she smiled in her sleep, as if some happy dream had come to her. So he kissed her very gently on the forehead, marvelling that the trumpet-calls, which grew swiftly nearer, disturbed her not, and whispered to her—

"Sleep sound, beloved, till the battle be overpast, and peace, the peace of victory, welcome thy waking."

Then for the last time he turned from

her, for peace was not yet, until Nothung
his sword had spoken sharp words with
its flaming tongue.   Swiftly he strode up
the rocky ridge, where the embattled
thunder-clouds swallowed him up, nor was
there any fear in his heart : only he longed
to see Hunding face to face, and drive
vengeance home.

But Sieglinde lay there smiling in her
sleep, for it was even as Siegmund had
supposed, and she was a child again living
with her mother in the forest.   Yet even
as Siegmund left her, the tranquillity of her
sleep was shaken, and it seemed to her
that her father and the boy Siegmund were
in the forest together, and though the hour
was late, they had not yet returned.   And
she cried to her mother that her heart
misgave her, for she was troubled with the
looks and the words of certain strangers.

Then in her dream the sweet air of the forest grew foul and black, and smoke swirled silently out of the woods, and tongues and fingers of flame came nearer, and the house where they dwelt caught fire. Then aloud she cried on Siegmund to save her, and with her own cry awoke. Yet was it not perhaps her own cry that woke her, but the sudden and sharp din of thunder near by, and starting up she saw she was alone, and all round her were storm-clouds of awful blackness, and from one to another shot the fires of lightning, and the thunder bellowed when it saw them. And mixed with the lightnings and thunders were the red cries of the horns of battle. Then, and her heart stood still when she heard, from not far off came the voice of Hunding, which she knew well and hated.

"Wehwalt, Wehwalt!" it cried, calling

her beloved by the name he had shed as trees shed their leaves in autumn. "Where are thou? Wait for me; I am coming swiftly; else shall my hounds make thee stay."

Then in answer came the voice she knew and loved; "Think not to hide from me, Hunding," it cried, "for all that the storm is so black and blinding. The father of the gods himself shall not hide thee from me. Stay where thou art and I will surely find thee."

And his voice grew louder as he spake, so she knew that he was coming nearer.

Then from the ridge close behind came Hunding's voice again, not a stone's-throw off, yet in the thick darkness she could see nought.

"O shameful wooer!" it cried. "In Fricka's hand is thy lot set."

And immediately Siegmund answered, being also come to the selfsame ridge—

"Still dost thou think I am weaponless, coward and fool that thou art? Thinkest thou to terrify me by thy woman-champion? Fight me, fight me. Remember thou the sword in thy house which none could move. Lightly I unsheathed it, and its tongue shall lick up thy life-blood; for thy life-blood it thirsts, and soon will I give it to drink."

Then came a flash of lightning from the cloud, and Sieglinde saw them as phantoms on the edge of the ridge already at fight. And she rushed towards it, not being able to bear that sight, calling loudly on them to stay, or first to kill her, and then settle their quarrel. But ere she was come to the ridge, a blinding light broke out of the cloud above the head of Siegmund, so strong and glorious that she was dazzled and fell back from before it. But in the middle of that light there appeared Brunnhilde floating there, and lo! her shield was held out so that it protected Siegmund and sheltered him. And she cried loudly to her hero, in a fierce merriment—

"Have at him, Siegmund ; thy sword is safe under my shield."

Then was Siegmund's heart uplifted, and he drew back his arm for a deadly stroke at Hunding, when even as it was about to fall, right over Hunding's head broke out a red and lurid light, full of wrath and anger, and in the midst stood Wotan, standing over the other, with his spear outstretched over against Siegmund. And in the voice at which all earth and heaven trembles—

"Thy sword is shivered, Siegmund,"

said he. "Wotan's spear is stretched against thee. Sink thou back from it."

Then did Brunnhilde quail in panic terror before her father, and her shield no longer covered Siegmund. And the mighty blow of his sword struck on that out-stretched spear and was shivered, and into his breast did Hunding thrust his sword, so that he fell and moved no more. And Sieglinde, beholding, gave one bitter cry, and sank swooning to the ground. But as Siegmund fell, the great light which had shone round Brunnhilde was swallowed up in darkness, and the red light round Wotan was extinguished also. And under cover of the darkness Brunnhilde, though stricken sore with the fear of the wrath of Wotan, yet was mindful of the woman Sieglinde, whom she had sworn to be-friend, and she stole down from the ridge

"Wotan's spear is stretched against thee, Siegmund."

crouching, yet firm of purpose, to her side.

" To horse ! to horse ! " she cried ; and seeing that Sieglinde's senses were gone from her, she gathered her up in the strength of her noble womanhood, and with that burden in her arms mounted her horse Grane and galloped off away from the open places that she might hide her from the wrath to come. Nor was she too soon, for presently after the clouds were parted and rolled away, and lo! on the ridge stood Wotan, and at his feet lay Siegmund. And as Wotan looked at him his godlike mind was torn with agony and woe unspeakable. As yet Hunding saw not the god, for his eyes were not opened, and cruelly with his foot on the man he wrenched out his sword from his breast. And at that, seeing that he who had fallen was noble, and the other

M

but a black cur from the forest, Wotan turned to him and opened his eyes.

"Get thee hence, slave," said he, "and tell Fricka that by the spear of Wotan is her vengeance wrought.   Begone!"

And in contempt he waved his hand, and before that withering scorn Hunding sank down dead.   Then suddenly fierce anger seized Wotan, for he thought of what Brunnhilde had done, and how she disobeyed his command, and made scorn of his words.

"Woe to her, woe to her!" he cried. "Dire and dread shall be her portion for this day's work.   With the reined lightning and the bridled thunder follow I after her, swift on the wings of the storm."

And at his word the winds of heaven and all the hurricanes of the air rushed to his bidding, and seated in his chariot of storms he drove on Brunnhilde's trail.

CHAPTER VIII

THE FLIGHT OF BRUNNHILDE

Now on that day on which Brunnhilde disobeyed the behest of Wotan, and instead of slaying Siegmund, and bringing his soul to Walhalla where he would abide with the other heroes, shielded him, yet to little purpose, the glorious company of the Valkyries, who were eight in number, and all her sisters, being likewise the daughters of Wotan and born of Erda, were out to battle and fight with the heroes of the sons of men, whom they bore to Walhalla, there to defend its lofty walls and sit at wine with their fellows.

All that day had they ridden on their quests, and when it was towards evening they began to gather, as they had appointed, on the top of a certain rocky height, there to number their spoils, and go all together, a wild and joyous company, to the halls of Walhalla, there to gladden the heart of their father Wotan with what they had done.

High and open to the winds of heaven was their trysting-place, a region of bleak mountain land, a very crown of the world. Steeply rose its barren cliffs on all sides but one, and here a pine wood clung to the hillside, in the shade and shelter of which they might tether their horses, as they waited for the gathering of their sisters. Great storms had raged all day, and as evening came on their violence was in no whit abated, but seemed to

grow ever fiercer. But little did the
Valkyries heed such menaces, for their
joy was in storm, and they drank deep
from whirlwinds as a thirsty man will
drink of a bowl of wine, and feel his
strength come back to him ; and the
swifter the blasts screamed over the
terror-stricken earth, the swifter did the
Valkyries ride on their errands, and the
louder and more joyous sounded their
fierce, glad battle-cries of death. High
and untamed of heart were they, and
maidens all of them, for of men they had
no thought, save only that men were the
game and quarry of their hunting, and
they loved a strong man's strength only
because thus the fighting was the fiercer,
and the nobler and braver was the foeman
whose soul they should carry to Walhalla,
there to have life eternal breathed into it

by Wotan. But of the fierceness of love
they knew nought, nor cared to know:
danger and death had brighter eyes for
them than a lover.

All day had their trysting-place stood
empty and buffeted by the winds and
rains, for far distant were the quests on
which the sisters had gone, and wild
and shrill was the music of the storm.
Now with a scream the wind would awake
and yell among the rocks, and the beating
of the rain was like the sound of the drums
that call to war. Then the shrillness of
the storm would abate, and for a while
it would moan with low and flute-like
notes among the stems of the pine-trees,
and whisper among their nodding tops, as
if with a false promise of peace. Then in
fresh anger, as of hounds a-yelp, it would
break out again, and with shrill trumpet-

ings scream among the sharp edges of the
rocks, or vibrate like to a twanged string
round the stumps of trees and weep like
some lost soul among the thick-stemmed
bushes.   But towards evening, though the
rain abated not, nor the mad riot of the
winds, a man might hear very far away
the rhythmical tramping of some deathless
steed, as one of the wild Valkyries
approached, or far away a light would
break out among the clouds showing
where another rode lightly on the very
winds and airs of heaven.   Thus flying
and galloping from every quarter of the
world, that glorious company began to
assemble, and the storm screamed welcome
to them with many voices.

Legion were the questions each had to
ask of the other, as to how she had sped
that day, and what hero she brought back

slung across her saddle-bows, and joyful were the greetings with which each hailed the other. Some, too, had brought with them the horses of the slain, and loud were the neighings and whinnyings in the wood as horse smelt filly, and cocked his ear and swished his tail for very joy of the life that was in him. But the noblest of all were the steeds of the Valkyries, and these they tied up to the trees while they waited for their full company to gather; and they cared for them tenderly, for it was by the deathless strength of their noble steeds that they rode so swiftly on their wide errands of death. Again and yet again flared the wild light of their approach, and on the saddle of each was swung a hero, for all had prospered that day, and joyfully they spoke together of the gathering there would be in Walhalla

that night when they returned triumph-
ant, and how Wotan would be well
pleased at their prowess ; while high rose
the mirth at the table where sat the heroes,
as their new brethren made whole again,
and filled with eternal life by the power of
Wotan, sat them down in wonder and
amaze at the glory and joy that awaited
them, when their eyes were opened after
the sleep of death, to behold the dawning
of the everlasting day.

And by now all the maidens were
gathered but one only, for Brunnhilde,
the eldest and the most noble of them
all, had not yet returned from her quest,
and the sisters wondered that she should
delay so long. But one, thinking that
they were all gathered, asked another
why yet they delayed, for the sun was
near its setting, and it was time they

set forth to go to Walhalla with their
spoils.

But she to whom her sister spake,
replied—

"Not yet are we all gathered, for
Brunnhilde comes not yet. Her deed
to-day, as I know, my sisters, was with
the Wolsung Siegmund, and she tarries
long, for he fights for a woman, and men
in such case are ever fiercest. Yet may
we not go to Walhalla till she is come, for
what welcome, think you, we should get
from Wotan, came we before him lacking
his heart's darling? Dear are we all to
him, but she is the dearest, and to us the
dearest of all is she."

Meantime another of the eight, Siegrune, had climbed to the topmost ridge
of rock, and looked out as best she might
through the blinding storm, to see if

Brunnhilde approached. Then suddenly the others below heard her shout of joyful war-cry, with which the sisters were wont to hail each other.

"She comes, she comes!" she cried, "and the speed of her coming is like the passage of the lightning, and as thunder the rides on the wings of the wind."

Then they all called aloud on her, and another sister, Waltraute, swiftly ran up to where Siegrune sat.

"See, she rides to the wood, and her good Grane labours sore. How spent he seems with her headlong speed."

And yet a third climbed up beside the two others.

"The wildest, fiercest ride that ever Brunnhilde sped," she cried. "But see! what lies on her saddle? No hero is it."

Then as the maid came nearer, riding

on the wings of the storm, they saw that it was no hero indeed she carried, but a woman ; and swiftly they hurried down to the wood to meet her, for that a Valkyrie should bring back a woman as spoil was in truth a new thing.   And as they ran down they questioned one with another what this could be.   They saw, too, that her good horse Grane was utterly spent with the gallop, and this, too, was a new thing, for Grane had the stoutest heart and the most untiring limbs of any horse in earth or heaven.

Then came Brunnhilde towards them through the trees, giving her support and strength to the woman Sieglinde, whom she led.   Round her neck was Sieglinde's arm laid, yet scarcely even so could she put foot before foot, for like Grane the strength of her body was spent utterly,

Brunnhilde brings Sieglinde to the Valkyries' Meeting-place.

and her soul was sore with all that had come upon her. Then with hands outstretched in entreaty came Brunnhilde to them ; and that, too, was a strange thing and a new, for of them all she was the blithest.

" Save me, sisters," cried she, " for harm follows hard after me, and I who never yet fled from any man fly now, and behind me in thunder and relentless pursuit follows the War-father."

And down she sank on a seat of rock, still supporting her whom she led.

But wonder and amazement seized on the sisters, and it seemed that she must be distraught and her wits astray that she spoke so, for how should Wotan, whose darling she was, and whose very will she mirrored, be up in wrath against her?

Then Brunnhilde cried out again—

"Run to the topmost ridge, my sisters, and tell me if ye see aught. Look to the northward and say if the father comes, and if he is yet in sight, for I have fled before him. All day I have fled before him, and my heart is gone from me, for he rides furiously."

Then did the sisters do her bidding, and lo! to the northward there rose in the sky a great cloud, separate from the storm down which Brunnhilde had steered, and it rose high and black and moved very swiftly, and out of the midst of it came thunderings and lightnings, nor could they doubt but that this was Wotan riding on the clouds, his chariot. Then returned they and told Brunnhilde what they had seen, and she was very sore afraid, for she too knew that fast in pursuit came Wotan from the north, and that he came in

wrath and terrible anger.   And again she
cried—

"Save me, my sisters, and shield the
woman.   Ye know not who she is, but I
will tell you all and quickly, for there is no
time to lose.   Sieglinde is it I bring, the
sister of Siegmund the Wolsung and his
bride.   Wotan this day, for Fricka's sake,
doomed to death the Wolsung, and bid
me forsake him whom ever I had loved.
And obey I could not, for my heart
allowed me not, and instead of forsaking
him, and fighting against him, I sheltered
him with my invincible shield.   But on
the other side fought Wotan, and against
his spear was Siegmund's sword shattered.
Then fear seized me, and I fell back, so
that my shield no longer sheltered him,
and by Hunding's sword did Siegmund
fall.   And with this woman fled I before

N

the wrath that is coming, and hither I came, for with your help maybe the fulness of his displeasure shall be turned from my head."

Then were all the sisters filled with sorrow and amazement that she had disobeyed the word of Wotan, and scarce could they believe that she had dared to do this thing, for that Wotan's word should not be obeyed was a thing unthinkable, and they were sorely grieved. And ever from the north, like night, came the storm-chariot of Wotan nearer, and they knew the growing roar of the thunder to be the whinnying of the wild horses that he drove.

But Brunnhilde looked on Sieglinde, and as she looked all fear for herself was merged in pity for her, and again she spake to her sisters.

"Sisters, sisters, woe and destruction

waits this woman if she abides the coming
of Wotan, for with fire and wrath and the
utmost terror of his face he wars against
the Wolsungs. So, for my horse Grane is
spent, lend me, I pray you, one of yours,
that with her I may flee again and make
her safe."

Then, though they all loved Brunnhilde,
and she entreated each in turn, yet none
would do this, for Wotan was their father,
and not even at Brunnhilde's prayer could
they turn from him. Thus she knew not
which way to turn for help, and she bent
over Sieglinde, and for pity of her and for
sorrow she kissed her and embraced her
lovingly. And at that caress Sieglinde,
who till now had taken no part or lot in
this wild war of words, but had sat as one
who saw not nor felt, looked up into
Brunnhilde's eyes, and saw all the sorrow-

ful loving-kindness which sat there, and made such softness in her eyes.

"It is enough," she said, "for death, now Siegmund is dead, terrifies me not at all, and I would not that harm came to thee for my sake. Would that some blow in that strife had fallen on me, so that I might have died with him. Indeed I will not be parted from him. So, O thou holy and dear maiden, who hast been so tender to me, let me not live and curse thy tenderness, but hearken to my prayer, and strike me to the heart with thy sword. Strike strongly of thy strength."

And Brunnhilde spoke low to her and earnestly. "Ah, not so, not so," she said. "Cast not his love away, the pledge of which he has given thee. For hidden deep in thee lies another life; from thy womb shall spring a Wolsung."

Then did the mother awake in the woman, and all her face was flushed as with sunrise by a holy joy. Though she had no fears for herself, yet it could not be that the begotten of Siegmund should perish, and she thought of her unborn babe.

" Ah, save me and shelter me," she cried, "and shelter my helpless babe. O, ye maidens, I call you to save me and hide me from the wrath of Wotan."

Then suddenly came the voice of Waltraute from the topmost rock. " The storm is at hand," she cried. " Get thee hence, ere it fall on thee."

At that the others cried to Brunn-hilde to get hence with the woman, for they dare not ward her from Wotan, and Sieglinde fell on her knees, and as mother of a child that should yet be born, besought Brunnhilde to save her for the sake of her motherhood that should be.

Then did Brunnhilde commune swiftly with herself, for lacking a horse she could not hope to flee with the woman before the face of Wotan. Yet when she spake her voice trembled, for she was afraid. But by no other way could she save Sieglinde and that holy seed.

" Get thee away alone," said she, " and flee softly and swiftly from the wrath. But I abide here so that in wrath against me he may delay his further pursuit. Here and on me will that full flood break, and here will it pour itself forth, and in the meantime shalt thou make thyself safe against his pursuit."

And for the sake of her child, Sieglinde pressed her hands in thanks.

"And whither shall I flee from the wrath?" she asked.

Then Brunnhilde turned again to her sisters. "O help me here," she said, "for in this in no way do ye cross the will of Wotan. Say, which of you have journeyed eastward this day?"

And Siegrune answered: "I, and eastward lies there a great wood where the giant Fafner guards the ring which was made from the Rhine-gold. That none should know it is he, he has taken the likeness of a mighty dragon, and in his lair he guards the ring. Yet it is no place for a helpless woman."

"Nor meet for a helpless woman is it to abide the wrath of Wotan," answered Brunnhilde. "And that wood, well know I, Wotan loves not, nor ever does he venture in its shade, for he thinks that there lurkes evil for him, and dark is the womb of fate."

Even as she spoke again, Waltraute shouted from the rock. "Wotan is very near," she cried ; " hear ye not the roar of his coming ?"

Then Brunnhilde trembled, but delayed not, and taking hold of Sieglinde she showed her the way she must follow.

" So begone!" she cried, "and set thy face ever eastwards. Great indeed is the burden that thou bearest within thee, so let thy heart be great also. Hunger and thirst will be thine, and the stony rock shall be thy bed, and with thorns shalt thou cover thyself, and of briars shalt thou make thy pillow. So be lifted up in thy courage and take these things blithely, and laugh only when thy need is the sorest. And, O woman! forget not ever, nor think lightly of what I tell thee, for within thee in the darkness of thy womb lies he who shall be the highest hero of earth."

Then took she from her mantle the fragments of the sword of Siegmund which she had gathered up when it was shattered against the spear of Wotan, and darkness fell on the rocky ridge where he fought with Hunding.

"Treasure these safe," said she, "for these are the shattered pieces of thy man's sword. Them gathered I for thy child, and he once more shall wield it in days to be. And I name him now. Siegfried shall he be, and by him shall be won the peace of victory, and the sword shall make him glad. So begone!"

But Sieglinde clung to her a moment yet.

"O, sweetest and most mighty of

maidens," she said, "thy truth to me has made me believe that what thou now sayest is to be.   That which thou hast given me, which was his whom we both loved, I will guard very jealously, and by him who will spring from Siegmund's loins perchance shall one day thy sorrow and mine be turned into joy and laughter.   So farewell.   The woman of many woes and sorrows blesses thee every day and for ever."

Then she went swiftly away eastwards through the pines.

CHAPTER IX

THE SENTENCE OF BRUNNHILDE

For a moment Brunnhilde stood there watching with a strange exaltation the figure of Sieglinde as it grew ever dimmer in the dimness of the plumed pines, and when it was now quite vanished she turned again, and stood yet awhile with clenched hands and knitted brow, so that she might be mistress of herself when the heavy wrath of Wotan fell on her, and disgrace not her own nature nor the bright company of her fearless sisters. Little she seemed to care what doom he might mete out to her, for at the worst he

could but deal her swift death, and if the
sons of men could die bravely and blithely,
meeting the face of death as they would
meet a friend's face, could she do less, she
the first of the children of Erda ? For
all that, she was afraid, and with her fear
there cut her like a two-edged sword
the pang of remorse that she had disobeyed him whom her soul loved. Yet in
this matter she knew well that were that
choice again before her, she would do again
as she had done, and not otherwise, for
pity had enlightened her, and that sweet
mandate was binding on her.

Then lifted she her eyes and saw that
the height where her sisters had watched
was already quite hidden by the thunder
clouds that had driven so swiftly from the
north, and it was as if black night encom-
passed the place. And from the middle

of the cloud came the unceasing roar of thunder and the wild lanterns of the lightning flashed all ways at once. Then for a moment they ceased, and out of the middle of the cloud came the voice she loved, and it was more terrible than all the thunderings. Not very loud was it, but therein lay wrath as deep as the sea, and unappeasable as the desert's thirst ; and it called her by name. And when Brunnhilde heard that she stood very still.

But the other Valkyries wailed among themselves when they saw that their father Wotan had even now reached the place, and loudly they bewailed for their sister Brunnhilde, for by his voice they knew that Wotan was exceedingly wroth. Then suddenly at the sound of their wailing, the fountains of fear were altogether loosed within Brunnhilde, and she felt sick with very terror, and her knees shook together. And she who had never besought aught for herself, besought them now.

"Sisters, sisters of mine, help me!" she cried, "for the sickness of fear has come upon me, and my heart is pierced. Surely his rage will crush me utterly, if you protect me not. Stand round me, let me hide among you, that he come not on me alone."

Then were her sisters full of pity for her, for none could 'gainsay or resist her appeal; and in a company they ranged themselves upon a little rocky height that was there, all eight of them, and Brunn-hilde they set in their midst, and she cowered down among them. Thus it might be that Wotan would suppose that she had not joined her sisters in fear of his displeasure, and that thus he might seek her elsewhere. And they whispered to her to be of good cheer, and crouch low in the midst of them, and not answer to his call. This she did; and they grouped themselves round her on the rocky point, and thus awaited the coming of Wotan. Yet the bravest of them were afraid at the thought of the wrath that was coming, for they had seen him alight from his chariot on the mountain-top close above them, and in the calm of his anger there was that which was more terrible than the bellowing thunder or the lightning stroke. Then without haste came he down and stood before them. In his right hand he held the ashen spear, and his left hung by his side with fingers clenched, and his glorious face, before which the earth trembled, was very still and set; only the point of his spear trembled like an aspen leaf as he held it, and the Valkyries knew the wrath that shook him. Then he opened his mouth and spake very gently.

"Where is Brunnhilde?" said he, "for after her and her wickedness am I come. Do you think to hide her from me, or that ye will veil her and her evil deed from the reward I mete out to it?"

Then one and another replied to him, hoping to turn away his wrath; and one said that nought that she could do was so terrible as the anger with which he sought her; and another asked what it was that had so moved his rage; and yet another spake of the heroes they had slain that day, thus vainly seeking to cool his anger. But to their replies he answered not; only the trembling of the head of the ashen spear grew more violent, and at the last

he broke out, no longer being still and
calm in his wrath, but with an outburst of
such rage as they had not dreamed was
there. For all that, it was not so terrible
as the stillness of the anger in which he
had come to them.

" Is it your purpose to mock me ? " he
cried. " Indeed I am not good to mock.
O, ye Valkyries, ye wax over-bold, nor
does this delay serve to calm my displeasure, but it spreads further like the
rising tide, and reaches you too. Of what
avail then are your idle words? for well
I know that there in your midst ye
foolishly seek to guard Brunnhilde. I
bid you all then to stand off from
her, for from me and from you and
your company she is for ever an outcast. She has proved herself worthless.
Worthless is she, and the doom of the

o

worthless shall come upon her at my hands."

Then again once more they besought him, for they trembled for Brunnhilde who in their midst lay trembling, and they told him how in panic of fear she had fled before him, beseeching her sisters to shield and shelter her, for they knew that they could not deceive him, nor was it of any use to say that she was not with them. So ere they handed her to him they tried to soften his anger, telling him that already fear, like some ploughshare, had furrowed her heart, that heart which had never yet trembled nor turned faint. Then with one voice they besought him to have pity, remembering her mighty deeds. But their pleading but more inflamed him, for it was the very darling of his soul who had disobeyed him, and thus her sin was the more grievous, and to try to turn his wrath and beseech in this sort seemed to him a womanish deed. So again he broke out in ever fiercer anger.

"Are ye indeed Valkyries?" he said, "and can it be that I have begotten a brood so timorous of soul, and so little courageous? Women of faint heart are ye all! Were these the hearts that I moulded, which should meet war and the clash of fighting like men, sharp as steel and hard as tempered steel, that like a pack of women you whimper in this sort when I, the righteous judge, come to visit one who has failed in truth? Ah! and ye know not half."

For a moment his anger all died out and left him only very sorry, for he loved Brunnhilde with a love far deeper than any of her sisters could ever know, and his voice softened.

"Ye shall hear what she has done," he said, "and judge if it was not meeter that my tears should flow and that I rather than you should weep and wail. For to her, to Brunnhilde, my innermost being and the secrets of my heart were known as to myself, and into her soul, as into a well of water, I looked and beheld myself, and my will that had been dark to me grew clear. In her, as in the womb of a woman with child, my will matured, and from her it came to birth. Never was there love like this between any man and maid. Was that a bond to lightly loose ? Yet to-day she loosed it, and she who was my will fought against me. A clear command I laid on her, and in the sight of heaven and earth she disobeyed it, and the sword of

*Crouching among
her sisters.*

Siegmund, made by me, was directed against myself by her command. She has done this."

Then he paused a little space, and again he spoke : " No longer I speak to you Valkyries, I speak to her. Dost thou hear me, Brunnhilde ? Thou whom in every part I fashioned, to whom I gave thy deathless armour, to whom I gave all the sweetness and joy of life, dost thou hear me ?   And hearing me, art thou, thou, Brunnhilde, afraid, that thou hidest thyself like a coward, thou, Brunnhilde, and would shrink away from the doom and punishment that I have appointed for thee ? So come out, come out, and of thy own free-will ! "

And when Brunnhilde, crouching among her sisters, heard the voice of her father speaking in such sort to her, him whom she knew best and loved best of all the world, all fear suddenly died in her heart, for the love that each had towards the other cast fear out, and she knew only that he called her, and she must go. And she stood up straight, and with her hands to right and left she parted the sisters who would have screened her still, and with firm step and head borne proudly, as was ever her wont, she came near to where Wotan stood and looked him in the face and spoke to him.

"Father, I am here," she said. "Make known to me what thou willest."

Then answered Wotan : "Not from me, Brunnhilde," he said, "comes thy fate ; it is thou thyself who hast sent it. Was it not by the might of my will that thy soul first awoke in thee ? Yet thou hast warred against thy own soul. It was the might of my word that made thee mighty in noble deeds, yet to my word thou hast given the lie.   Thou wast ever the maiden of my will to me, and against my will hast thou gone.   Thou wast the maiden who bore my shield, but against me hast thou stretched the shield forth.   It was thou whom I appointed to choose the lots of life and death.   Where I ordained life thou didst think to give death, where I appointed death thou didst let live.   It was thou whom I appointed to lift up the hearts of heroes, yea, and thou didst lift them up against me.   I tell thee all that thou wert ; but by what name thou shouldest now be called, thou knowest thyself. No more art thou the maiden of my will, but maiden only, and as Valkyrie thou hast gone on thy last errand.   From henceforth thou art that which thou hast

made thyself; thou metest out thy own
punishment, and it is just."

Then did it seem to Brunnhilde that
she could have borne all else but only this,
that she should be thus parted from her
father, and her heart was stricken.

" Dost thou so cast me from thee ? " she
said.   " Canst thou think to do such a
thing ? "

" Thou sayest it," said he, " and thou
art outcast from me utterly.   Never again
from Walhalla shalt thou storm forth at my
bidding on thy joyous errands, nor ever
again shall I show to thee the heroes thou
shalt fight and slay, guiding their souls at
eventide to my halls, there to make merry
at the joyful feastings of the gods.   Nor
ever again when the mirth grows louder,
deep into the night, shalt thou hand me the
wine-cup, nor again shall our souls mingle

in the sweet caresses of father and daughter as was our wont. For out of the company of gods thou art taken, and thy place shall know thee no more, and thou, that fair flower-bud that grew so strong and sweet on the abiding stem of my godhead, art nipped off and cast away. For the bond between us is broken, and for ever art thou banished from before my face, and out of the light of mine eyes."

Then began the sisters all to weep and to wail, for like Wotan they loved her, and with words of pity they called on her by name, and bitterly they lamented themselves. But among them all Brunnhilde stood dry-eyed and firm. Nought said she to vainly try to turn his mind, she wished but to learn her uttermost doom.

" Then is all, all that thou hast given

me, utterly lost to me?" she said. "Of all thy gifts dost thou strip me? Is all lost to me?"

"Yea, and it is lost to me," said Wotan, "for from the life and light of the gods thou passest. Here shalt thou abide, even here, and deep sleep shall wrap thee round, and thou shalt be alone and without protector, until the day come that some man, a wayfarer, passing here shall see a maid lying alone, and shall come to her and wake her, and she shall be his. Maiden only thou art, not maiden of my will, and to maid, as is fit, comes man."

But even now when the horror of her full doom was told to Brunnhilde, still she swooned not nor bewailed herself. But among the sisters again rose wild tumult and bewilderment of pity, for of all dooms to fall into the hands of a man was to them the most shameful, and the stain and disgrace that was decreed to her touched their sisterhood. And with one consent they entreated their father to have pity, and not put that uttermost degradation on her, but refrain from cursing her with so great an infamy. Yet he paid no heed to their wailings, for it was even as he said, and Brunnhilde was the maiden of his will no more, but a maiden only, and a man will find the maiden at the last.

Then because they still importuned him till he was vexed with them, he turned fiercely on them. "Her fate is fixed," he cried, "and ye have heard it. From you as from me is she for ever separate because she was faithless; and as I have said, so shall it be. No more

shall her steed whinny to its fellows as
ye fly together on the wings of the winds.
And here shall she abide till the man who
fares by shall pluck the full bloom of her
sleeping maidenhood, and from maid shall
make of her mother.   To man her master
shall her heart be bent, and meekly shall
she do all his will.   The cares of the house
shall be hers, and by the hearth-side shall
she sit and ply the distaff, as befits a wife,
and the mockers among men, it may be,
shall make merry at her.   Woman shall
she be among the sons of men, and her
fate none other than theirs."

Then was the spirit of Brunnhilde
broken within her, for the punishment
was harder than she could bear; yet still
she said no word.   But her sisters again
broke out into lamentations, whereat
Wotan was angry, for what must be,

must be, and their bewailings were but a waste of breath and cowardly withal. Nor was it his will to palaver longer with them.

"Begone, begone!" he cried, "for but a little more and ye share her doom. So begone, lest her fate be yours also. For the last time ye look on her face. And should one of you remain here lingering, in vain hope of resisting my will or changing my unchangeable mind, Brunnhilde's doom is hers too. So be wise while there is time. Get ye gone from this rock, her sleeping-place, and let none again be found here. To horse with you all, for swiftly shall woe light on the loiterer."

Then the sisters, seeing that the doom was spoken, and though Walhalla should fall, yet should Wotan's word abide, went very sorrowfully to their horses, and loosed them from their tetherings, and each mounted and rode off. Shrill through the woods and the echoing mountain-side sounded the storm of their going, for the winds awoke to speed them, and over dale and down glen they sped swiftly, till the noise of their travel grew faint, and on the mountain-side there abode only Wotan and Brunnhilde, who still lay crouched at his feet.

The flight of the Valkyries.

CHAPTER X

THE SLEEP OF BRUNNHILDE

THUS the wild storm of the ride of
the Valkyries passed away. Like smoke
they were borne away on the wings of
the tempest, and a windless calm fell
round about the place where Wotan and
Brunnhilde abode on the mountain-top.
The sun was already set, though still to
westwards there lingered the reflected
fires of its setting, and star by star
came out in the deepening vault of blue
overhead, until all heaven was spangled
with their burning and grew bright at
eventide. Eastward rose the moon at its

fullest, to climb its silent and appointed journey over the firmament, and shone with a light exceeding bright and clear as running water. In the brake the chorus of birds was hushed, and over hill and valley spread and deepened the spring night. Such a night indeed it was as that on which, but one sunset ago, had Siegmund come to the house of Hunding through the storms which day-long had lashed the hillsides; and now, even as then, the storm was hushed, and deep peace lay over the earth. Yet swiftly the finger of fate had written, and swift had been the accomplishment of that decree, for lover lay dead and husband also, while through the gloomy forest hurried Sieglinde eastwards, to shield that which lay within her from the wrath of Wotan. And she, Brunnhilde, that

had befriended the lover and his beloved,
lay very still at the feet of her father
making a darkness for her eyes, for on her
head had the wrath come, and stern and
terrible was her punishment. For lightly
had she recked of his godhead and his
holy behest, and by the maiden of his
will had his will been betrayed; thus
she was will-maiden to him no longer,
and should wayfarer hap on her, not
maid but woman, for so had the word
gone forth from Wotan's mouth. Long
time then sat the god there motionless
with the crouched figure of her he loved
at his feet, but at the last she raised her
head, and essayed to meet the eyes that
met not hers, and slowly she spoke.

"Is in truth my fault so vile and
shameful," said she, "that with so shameful a visitation thou must needs reward

it? Time was when high on the sunlit
cliff of godhead I stood with thee, and
have I now by my sin cast myself down
so utterly to the slime and horror of the
nethermost pit, that viler phantoms than
Hella ever knew must flap their wings
of darkness round me? Surely it is not
possible that in one moment I so put off
all the worth that ever was mine, all
which I had from thee, that a fate so
unworthy fits me."

Yet still the god looked not at her,
and Brunnhilde nigh despaired. Yet
alone with him, for the twain were
indeed not two but one, she could
beseech and entreat him, though before
her sisters she thought shame to do so,
and slowly the words were wrung from
her, like dropping blood from some deep-
welling wound.

"Father, father!" she cried, "look once again in mine eyes, and let the light of thine dwell once more on my face, and search it well and remember what has been, and let not the loving-kindness of old days be forgotten. So, maybe, shall thy wrath not burn so fiercely against me, and thy anger be assuaged. Cast the strong and clear light of thy knowledge on the sin I have committed, and look well at it to see if indeed it merits this doom, so that thy child must be for ever forsaken by thee, and her love no more brought to remembrance."

Then looked he at her, but no ray shot across the sombre gloom of his face.

"Look at thy sin thyself," said he, "and let thy mind be to thee a lantern that illumines it. Mark it carefully, and know

fully indeed what thou hast done.   What
need for me to tell thee.   Thou knowest."

Then did Brunnhilde ponder on all they
had said together the night before con-
cerning the Wolsungs, and how Wotan's
mind ere yet he had talked with Fricka
had been to save Siegmund and destroy
Hunding, for he was husband to Sieglinde
only by name and vow, while Siegmund
was the man she loved, and how he had
commanded herself to fight well for
Siegmund.

" Time was," she said, " when thou wert
on Siegmund's side, and by thy side was I,
as ever.   It was the word that thou saidst
to me then which was in my heart when I
fought for him."

But the cloud moved not from Wotan's
face, but sat throned there heavily.

" Hotfoot from speech with me thou

wentest to the battle," said he. "Was
the word of mine that then rang in thy
ears to do as thou didst do?"

"Yet when first the lot was cast," said
the maid, "the lot of death declared for
Hunding."

"It was so," said he. "But the
bidding I gave thee then I revoked, and
thou knowest it. Yea, and thou didst
know it even when the sin of disobedience
was red upon thee."

"But who changed the mind that erst
was in thee?" said she. "Of thyself
thou didst not change it, but Fricka in-
clined thee to her will, breaking asunder
the resolve that thou hadst made. Her
whim it was that swayed thy mind; nor
was I the first foe to thy will, but thou
thyself, when the unalterable word that
thou hadst spoken was changed and

twisted and made of nought because so the whim of Fricka would have it."

Then was Wotan even more sore at heart, for he had thought that Brunnhilde had known his will to the full, but with open eyes had disobeyed it. Yet this was worse, in that she thought him infirm of purpose and easily swayed, and here lay treason to him.

But she, though no word came from him, yet fathomed his thought, and to that unspoken thought made reply.

"Father, I am not wise as thou art," she said, "but this I knew, that thou didst love the Wolsung who sprang from thy loins, and I thought that thy strife of words with Fricka had blinded thy mind and bewildered thy sense, so that in that moment thou wast unmindful of him. And it was a bitter thing to my heart to see Siegmund stand unprotected and outside the range of thy protecting arm, for thou didst ever love him, and in nought had he disobeyed thy word; though to Fricka's mind he had done amiss."

But Wotan's face still gloomed above her.

"Ah, thou didst know, thou didst know what way my choice had gone, and that which determined me concerned thee not," he said; "and knowing that, thou wert at Siegmund's side with the guard and shelter of thy shield, thou didst range thyself against me and against the word that had gone forth from my lips."

Then Brunnhilde knew there was only one thing left as yet unspoken by her by which might the doom that he had decreed upon her be averted. So that last

arrow left in her sheaf she drew. For
ever Wotan had been a friend to love,
whether among the gods or among the
race of men whom his might sustained
and his pity upheld. So now, since for
the first time the comprehension of love
had reached her, when that morning she
saw Siegmund recked nought of what
might be done to him, but considered
only that he might not be bereft of
his wife Sieglinde, and thus thought
scorn of Walhalla's blisses, if so be she
was not there to share them with him, so
Brunnhilde thought that even now at the
last Wotan might perchance pity her for
that which he knew so well, for the sake
of the love to which he was ever friend.

"It is true, it is true," she said, "but
there is yet one thing thou dost not know.
For when at thy bidding I first drew near

to Siegmund bearing swift death for him,
and having no thought in my mind of
pity for him or of disobedience to thy word,
my soul was melted when I saw how it
was with him, and heard him speak.
Then knew I that he was a hero, for no
fear at all was his, neither of swift bright-
eyed death, nor even of Hella itself, and
knew I also that one overmastering need
beset his soul, and that was his love for
Sieglinde. And my heart made obeisance
to his love, and reverenced it, and hence
was pity born. Behold, his tongue was
a trumpet, and the grief that was his he
blared forth, and none heard him but I.
The splendid sorrow of love that reached
as high as the heavens had in his heart
its everlasting seat, and that love throned
there thought scorn of all else, and to
the terrors with which I threatened him

his ear was utterly deaf. These things, father, I heard and saw, and as I hearkened and beheld, the might of that defenceless man shook the fortress walls that until then had ever girded my heart, and they tottered and fell, and lo! I was open to the invader. Thy godhead and thy nature that is mine, died, and as a maiden of mortal birth and human sufferings I stood before him, lost in one thought, how could I help him."

Again she made pause and drew closer to Wotan's knee.

"Father, who had given me the love that then burned in my breast?" she whispered. "Was it not thy will, thy will which had bade me guard the Wolsung? Indeed, so it seemed to me, it was thy will, and, even though it agreed not with the word that thou didst give me, was it not thy will that even then directed me against thy word ? "

But though all the anger had burned out of the face of Wotan, yet was it still stern and set like a mask of marble. And when Brunnhilde had done:

" Hast thou aught more to say, my daughter ? " he asked, and her silence answered him.

Then said he—

" Listen once again then, before we make an end. Love seems to thee then a light thing that thou canst turn to it so, for thou dost not know aught of its flames and its sorrows as I know them. Nor dost thou know, thou whom I thought ever to be the maiden of my will, how I myself sided against myself, and of the secret pangs and agonies that were mine. Ah, Brunnhilde, I have suffered, I have suffered ; faint I have often been and wounded, and wants that I cannot quench, and wishes that I cannot bridle have brought me to this, that my will wavers. Here is the wreck of my world, here is to me a grief that will not sleep. And thou for a worldly love—and herein is thy crime —hast choked the well of my love for thee. For in that love I rested and was content, for delight and laughter have been thy food, and deep thou hast ever drunk of our love which was untainted with the human passion and hunger which now thou callest love. In that and in thee found I my solace and rest, when the strife of the gods made me bitter and of uneasy heart. For dark settles around us, and black wings of fate but dimly seen hover near. And thou, in this hour, by thine own choice, thou hast deserted and forsaken me.

Thou hast chosen thine own way when
my will was otherwise.   Thus it is of thy
own choice that our parting draws nigh,
and no more may thy nature mix with
mine, nor ever again shall we hold sweet
converse together touching things high
and great, dealing wisely with them in
loving whispers. Thou thyself hast chosen;
therefore must I henceforth work without thy help and communion, and while
life and light endure, no more shall our
hearts leap towards one another in joyous
greeting."

Meantime while they talked together
had the full moon of spring risen high into
the night, and Brunnhilde with heart that
wandered for a moment from its woes
bethought herself, as she looked on the
earth she so loved, that never again would
she see it with eyes of sight divine.   And

like an echo from far off it came upon her
that even now high in Walhalla were the
tables for feasting set, yet all were waiting
till Wotan should come. Soon he would
come, but sorrowful and alone, and all
would see that her place was empty for
aye, and that another filled the wine-cup
and handed to the heroes the joy of the
grape. All this she was to leave, and her
untamed heart once more bid her make a
last effort, to see if not even now could she
not turn Wotan from his purpose. For at
the first the doom had so stunned her that
she could not believe it was for her, but
now under the calm and sweet night that
unreality of horror began to take shape,
and it was then no phantom. So once
more she turned to him.

"Worthless hast thou found me and
foolish," she said, "and altogether un-

profitable. For the word which thou didst give me I scarce could believe was thine. Yet what of the years that went before, when all thy teaching to me was to love what thou lovest ? "

But Wotan answered not, nor was his face moved, and again, in agony of the loneliness that was coming on her, she embraced his knees and cried to him—

" Is it so, then ? Are we parted utterly, and shall our joyous meetings be seen no more ? For lo! thou dividest that which is one and undivisible, and tearest away with a stroke a part of thine own self, yea, thine own heart thou castest aside. Ah, father, great father, forget not that this, this maid of thine, was part of thyself, her life thine, her all, thine. But now thou cuttest it off, thou thrustest me from thee, and if that must be, is it not enough ? But wilt thou desecrate this part of thee further, and shame it as thou hast said? That shame thou thyself wilt share. The fault was mine, but if thou doest as thou hast said, making me the toy of men and food for their sport and laughter, what a fall is there. And my fall is thine also."

Then answered he: "Thou hast chosen love to be thy master, and love thou hast lightly followed like some feathered line. It is fit then that thou follow the man who brings love to thee."

Then at the thought that she might fall a victim to some coward and craven fellow, some bloodless braggart, again she besought him that at the least he would promise her that the man who should win her might be worthy of her, a man of deeds and of bravery, even as her own bravery he knew was matchless, and her own deeds

many. For great was her fall even so, since
for the blisses of Walhalla, and the endless
joys of sharing in her father's work and
wisdom, she walked the earth, the wife of
a man. But if such man was a coward
and the scorn of men, the doom was not
to be borne.

But Wotan's face was marble still, and
he said only that she had turned from
him, nor could he make choice for her any
more.

Then since he might not choose for her,
Brunnhilde made choice, if so be that her
choice found favour in his eyes, and she
said—

" There lives on earth, father, the race
which thou thyself didst beget, and of that
blood, since it is thine, can never a coward
be born. And not far off is the day, when
from that race shall be born the noblest

hero that the world shall ever know. Him name I, of the Wolsung blood."

Then again there was anger in Wotan's eyes as he answered—

"Speak to me not of Wolsungs," said he, "for from them as from thee, and in the self-same hour, I have parted and withdrawn myself, and my love no longer goes before them, but hard after them follows and shall follow my hate. Already by it have they been hunted even to the death."

Then did Brunnhilde, that nothing should be concealed between them, tell him that by her hand was Sieglinde safe, the mighty mother of a man that should be, in whose veins ran the pure Wolsung blood, for Wolsung would be alike his father and his mother. And though Sieglinde fled in fear, yet in the appointed months would she bring forth him whom to save she fled.

Moreover Sieglinde bore with her, for she herself had given it, the sword which her father Wotan had granted Siegmund to find.

But when that sword was named, Wotan frowned and was afresh displeased, for in this had he sided against himself, and bitterness lurked in the thought.

" Broken is the blade thereof," he cried, "for against my spear which none may withstand was it shattered, and who shall make good such a shivering ? So speak not to me of swords. But now thy time has come, and though I have heard thee very patiently, for the love I bore thee, yet thou seest that it is but vain to seek to sway my mind from its course. So abide the lot which has fallen to thee, nor indeed have I the power to change it, for thou thyself didst prefer the love of man

to the love of Wotan, and what thou hast
done abides. Thy time has come, and I
must linger here with thee no longer, for
already I have lingered too long. Here
for the first time and the last must I turn
from thee, even as from me thou hast
turned. Nor may I learn what thou wish-
est, or knowing, may not perform. Thy
woe must I see fulfilled and accomplished."

"Then name it once again," said she,
" that I may hear my sentence."

And Wotan answered very solemnly—

" Here seal I thine eyes and thy limbs in
deep sleep," said he, "and sleep thou shalt,
till some one of the sons of men passes by
and wakes thee. His wife shalt thou be,
by right of finding."

Then Brunnhilde the Valkyrie spake for
the last time, and she fell on her knees
before the god.

"I rebel not, nor murmur," said she, "and
let the word thou hast spoken be done
unto me. I seek not to alter aught, but
in thy love grant me yet this. Grant me
this, ere the bands of sleep press down
my eyelids and swathe my limbs, that thou
wilt establish round my resting-place some
terror and hindrance that will affright the
coward and the falterer, so that none such
comes near me. Let him who wins me be
at least some hero of might, man, yet not
coward, for how could Brunnhilde mate with
such ? Let it be such a coming I wait, and
here unmurmuring will I fall asleep on this
height until he who comes awakes me.
Ah, father, father, grant me this boon, and
forbid it not, else with thy deathless spear
strike at me now, even as I cling to thy
knee. Blot me out and trample on me,
and let the winds scatter me over the

mountain-side, or the beasts devour me.
Better were that than to wither in the
arms of a coward. So leave me not un-
fenced against the approach of the worm
and the spider among men. So shall thy
word be fulfilled, and so shall I be saved
from the nameless horror. O bid fire to
be kindled and ring me round, and let the
red tower of flame make battlement and
ward for me on this rock. Set here fierce
tongues to affright the boaster, and let the
hot breath of the flame drive off the
empty braggart, who fears to face the
roaring of its rage. Grant me this. It is
finished."

Then for a long space did Wotan gaze
into her beseeching eyes, and thought
within himself of all the beautiful days
they had spent together, which now were
over and numbered with the unreturning

Then tenderly he
raised her from
where she knelt.

dead, and long he thought of the love they had ever had the one to the other until the day of her disobedience, and a mildness came over his almighty eyes, and he was fain to grant this boon to her, for in no way thus would his word be broken. Then tenderly he raised her from where she knelt, and once more his arm was round her neck, and her breath soft and sweet swelled and made full the bosom that beat close to his. So gazed she for the last time into his eyes, and when for the last time she heard his voice, it was tender and full of love, and all anger had gone from it as utterly as the spent storms had gone from the sky, and she knew that her boon was granted to her.

"Farewell," he said, "O noblest maiden, steadfast of heart. Thou holy solace in which my soul ever delighted, farewell,

farewell! Must I be ever far from thee and parted from thee, and shall I never more welcome thy coming which has aye been honey to me? Never any more must our horses range together as we ride, nor will it be thy hand but another's that gives the wine-cup to me. Many days of love have we spent together, and now I leave thee, thou delight and laughter of my eyes. Yet never has bride had for her bridal so glorious a beacon as shall burn for thine, for presently at my word will the flame ring here thy rock, and spread its flambent and deadly embrace to affright the coward, and thus none but the courageous of heart shall dare to vault the fence that shall guard thee. To one only shall it be granted to do this thing, and he is the man who is free with a freedom that I, Wotan, know not."

But when Brunnhilde heard his word she lifted her face to him, and Wotan kissed her, and her eyes sought his in the last look of all.   And brokenly came Wotan's speech, for he loved her ; and he kissed her on her sweet mouth and on her eyes.

" Often thus have we done, Brunnhilde," said he, " and often have thine eyes been closed under my kisses, and bright they have been when I kissed them, for the light of coming battle that shone there. Often too has the song of thy mouth, ere yet thou wert of age to go forth to fight, been wine to the souls of my hero-warriors. O eyes of thine, stars to me from a starry heaven, beacons to which my heart was often lifted strong with hope, when I worked upwards from gross bewilderment of darkness to this joyful and beauteous world !   Sweet physicians of my soul, for the last time ye heal me as my lips linger on you still.   Happier than I is he who next meets them, for on me no more is shed their guiding light.   Thus, even thus, I pass from thy side, and in my last kiss thy godhead steals back from thee to him who gave it birth."

And even as he spoke, and as on her eyes and mouth the god's lips were pressed, her eyes closed softly, and her mouth was shut, and softly she sank untroubled, and like a child tired with play, into his encircling arm.   And softly did Wotan take her up in his strong grasp, and softly and very tenderly he laid her on a low mossy bank that had spread its velvet beneath the shade of a whispering pine.   Then looked he the last time on her peaceful and sleeping face, and raising her head he put there her helmet, and shut down the vizor, so

that none could see her face. Then he
looked once more, now that her face was
gone from him, at the gentle swell of the
bosom of maidenhood, and at all the beauty
and strength of her tireless limbs ; and
then took her steel shield and laid it on
her body, and her spear he laid lightly on
her outstretched arm. Thus all his work
with her was accomplished, and there re-
mained only that he should fulfil the boon
which he had granted her ; and with firm
step he went a little space away and called
with loud voice on Loge, the flickering
god of fire.

" Loge, hear ! " he cried, " and arise and
come hither obedient to my hand. Come
thou in waves of fire, and encompass the
rock where I stand with thy burning.
Loge, Loge, up ! "

At that three times he smote the rock,

R

www.ingramcontent.com/pod-product-compliance
Lightning Source LLC
Chambersburg PA
CBHW030806020726
47499CB00006B/1785